"It's them," Cindy gasped. "They've come to take me."

A moment later Mrs. Lovell and a uniformed officer came into the house with Ian McLean on their heels.

"Hello, Cindy," the woman said. "We've found you a wonderful new foster home with a family in Lexington."

Cindy regarded her coldly. "I'm not going anywhere."

"You are," Mrs. Lovell said firmly. "You're going to a safe place where there aren't wild horses running around and where you won't get into any mischief."

"It wasn't Pride's fault!" Cindy yelled. "It was mine. I just wanted to help. I'm not going!"

The officer knelt down in front of Cindy. "I have a court order," he said gently. "We have to obey it."

"No!" Cindy cried, tears streaming down her cheeks. "I won't go."

Mr. McLean went over to her. "You know we want you to stay, Cindy, but you'll have to go with the officer for now. We're going to straighten this out—I promise!"

A horrible scene followed as the officer and the caseworker loaded a screaming and crying Cindy into the back of the car.

Don't miss these exciting books from HarperPaperbacks!

Collect all the books in the THOROUGHBRED series:

THOROUGHBRED

SHINING'S
ORPHAN

JOANNA CAMPBELL

HarperPaperbacks
A Division of HarperCollins*Publishers*

J
CAM
(HORSES)

This is a work of fiction. The characters, incidents, and dialogues are products of the author's imagination and are not to be construed as real. Any resemblance to actual events or persons, living or dead, is entirely coincidental.

HarperPaperbacks   *A Division of* HarperCollins*Publishers*
10 East 53rd Street, New York, N.Y. 10022

12/12/01 Gift Lot

Produced by Daniel Weiss Associates, Inc., 33 West 17th Street, New York, New York 10011.

First printing: February 1995

Printed in the United States of America

HarperPaperbacks and colophon are trademarks of HarperCollins*Publishers*

10 9 8 7 6 5 4 3 2 1

SHINING'S
ORPHAN

1

"WELL, WE DID IT," CROWED SAMANTHA MCLEAN'S BEST friend, Yvonne Ortez, as they pulled up the long gravel drive of Whitebrook Farm, the Thoroughbred breeding and training farm where Samantha lived. When they stopped, Yvonne opened the back door and unhooked the garment bag that was hanging there. "We found your prom dress. It's absolutely perfect! Tor's going to love it!"

Samantha smiled. "I hope so."

She stepped out of her father's car, holding an assortment of smaller bags that contained some shoes and a slim evening handbag that complemented the deep jade green of the dress she'd just bought in Lexington. But in spite of her satisfaction at finding the perfect dress, she was sorry that Yvonne hadn't found anything for herself.

1

"What a gorgeous day," Yvonne said, taking a deep breath of the late spring air and gazing over the rolling green hills, and miles of white fence crisscrossing Whitebrook. "Perfect for a pleasure ride. Are you up for it? I'd love to take Sierra out, if it's okay with you, and I haven't seen Shining in a while."

Samantha's face lit up at the mention of her beloved filly. Shining had just won her first race, and Samantha could still feel the excitement of watching her horse win. "And you have to see the yearlings, too. They've grown so much." Then, not wanting to be distracted by her favorite subject, she added, "In the meantime, what are we going to do about your dress?"

Yvonne shrugged as they entered the small white cottage where Samantha lived with her father, Ian McLean, the head trainer at Whitebrook. She tossed her jet-black hair over her shoulder. "I'll think of something," she said. She followed Samantha upstairs to her bedroom.

Samantha sighed. Normally, she didn't like to shop for anything but riding clothes or equipment. But the prom, well, that was different. She'd actually enjoyed trying on all the new prom styles and deciding which one she looked best in. Yvonne, who loved to shop, hadn't been able to find the perfect dress to set off the dark, exotic looks of her Spanish-Navajo-English descent.

2

"Hey," Samantha said suddenly, seized with inspiration. "What about that gorgeous Spanish outfit your aunt sent you from New Mexico?"

Yvonne handed Samantha's prom dress to her and flopped onto the bed.

"Oh, I don't know. Maybe. I just can't believe we're finally going to our senior prom. The country club is going to be perfect."

Samantha sat down in the chair at her desk and smiled dreamily. "Yeah. It's hard to believe we're finally seniors. It seems unreal."

Yvonne nodded. "And then after the prom, graduation and the parties."

"Speaking of parties," Samantha said, "I've been thinking that I'd like to have a party, a pre-prom dinner party for the six of us. You, me, Gregg and Tor, and Maureen and her date."

"Sounds great!" Yvonne said, sitting up on the bed, her eyes sparkling. "I'll help you. We can make it really romantic. Candlelight, soft music, special food . . ."

"You're reading my mind."

They discussed the details for a few more minutes, then went out to the mares' barn to visit the horses. "Hey, look at this," Yvonne said, peering into Shining's stall. "One of the barn kittens is sleeping on Shining's back."

"That's Flurry. She really loves Shining," Samantha

said, smiling at the sight of the small gray kitten curled up on Shining's hindquarters. Shining was standing very still, as if not to disturb her small guest. Her delicate ears pricked when she saw Samantha, and she gave an affectionate nicker. Samantha let herself into Shining's stall, ran her hand over the sleeping kitten's coat, then scratched the filly behind the ears. In the afternoon sun Shining's deep roan coat gleamed with fine breeding and good health.

It hadn't always been that way. Samantha could still remember her horror when she'd first set eyes on the listless, neglected horse many months ago. It had taken countless hours of hard work and loving care to transform Shining into the sleek, healthy racehorse now standing before her. She'd carefully watched Shining's diet, struggled to help her overcome her distrust of people, and used all her skills as a trainer and rider to help Shining become comfortable on a racetrack again.

Samantha had been overjoyed when Ashleigh Griffen and Mike Reese, the owners of Whitebrook along with Mike's father, had given Shining to her. Shining was her first horse, but that was only one of the many reasons she was so special. Another important reason was that she was half-sister to Wonder, a retired champion racehorse who was now a broodmare. Ashleigh had saved Wonder from certain death when she was a foal, and Wonder and her talented

4

offspring had a very special place in Samantha's heart.

"You know," Samantha said softly to her horse, "I feel so proud whenever I think of you crossing that finish at Keeneland last month. You were wonderful."

Shining nodded her finely boned head up and down as if she understood. Flurry, jostled from her comfortable perch, woke up and stretched luxuriously before jumping onto Shining's hay net. From there she leaped to the stall partition. She gave herself a thorough cleaning in the late May sunshine that poured into the barn.

Samantha stepped out of the stall and continued down the aisle, checking on each horse. She stopped and looked at the twin month-old orphan foals that were in the stall next to Shining's. Their mother had died at birth, and the nurse mare who'd been with them had started having trouble nursing the hungry foals. Len, Whitebrook's longtime stable manager, was now hand-feeding them with a bottle. The foals hadn't taken to the bottle at first, and for a while it looked as if they might not even survive, but the gentle, older black man had a magic way with horses, and the foals were beginning to respond. One was a dark bay, the other a chestnut, and their dark, bright eyes gazed unblinkingly at Samantha as she crooned softly to them. For all they'd been through in their short lives, they seemed to be thriving. Len was taking good care of them. And Shining was too. She kept a constant watch over them.

Samantha slipped into the next stall, Fleet Goddess's, and fluffed up the straw. The tall, almost-black mare was one of Samantha's favorites. Samantha had groomed her and exercise-ridden her back when she was in training. Goddess had won several important races before she had been retired, including the last race of the Triple Tiara, an important series of races for fillies. She had already had a yearling who showed great promise and a two-month-old foal named Fleeting Moment. Fleet Goddess had been bred once again to Jazzman, one of Mike's stallions, who'd had an illustrious racing career before he had been retired to stud at the farm.

Samantha went on to the next stall and said a special hello to Wonder, a beautiful chestnut, also now retired from the track. It was easy to see from her intelligent, wide-set eyes and near-perfect conformation that she was a champion through and through. She and all of her offspring were co-owned by Ashleigh and Clay Townsend, who owned Townsend Acres, a prestigious breeding and training operation where Ashleigh had once lived with her family.

These days, people were treating Wonder with special loving care. She had gone into early labor and miscarried her last foal a couple of months earlier. Now she was in foal again after a mating with

Townsend Victor, a reputable stallion from Townsend Acres.

Wonder whuffed contentedly as Samantha ran her hand down the horse's sleek neck. "You're looking great, girl," she said.

She hoped with all her heart that everything would go smoothly with this foal. The farm had been through so much lately. Aside from Wonder's miscarriage, there had been Pride, Wonder's colt, who'd recently been retired from a winning racing career due to a twisted and ruptured intestine. It had taken a miracle—plus Ashleigh's and Samantha's hard work and love—for him to pull through. He'd been bred to a limited number of mares that spring.

After giving the barn a thorough inspection, Samantha and Yvonne waved hello to Ashleigh, Mike, and Mr. Reese, who were reviewing some notes in the farm office, and wandered out to the yearling paddock. They watched as two of their favorites, Mr. Wonderful, Wonder's yearling, and Precocious, who was out of Fleet Goddess, gamboled about. The sun glimmered off their brilliant coats as they ran, snorting and tossing their heads. Samantha couldn't wait until these two went into training.

She went over to a small paddock where Vic Taleski, Whitebrook's young groom, had just turned Sierra out to enjoy the afternoon sunshine. Sierra was a strong-willed horse who had never been suited to the racetrack. But Samantha had believed in the dark chestnut horse. She and her boyfriend, Tor, had helped Sierra find his niche as a steeplechaser. He'd won an important 'chase at Aiken in April.

The big horse whuffed importantly as she approached, and she reached out to pat him on the muzzle. In the next minute she jerked her hand away as Sierra took a mischievous nip. Samantha laughed. Sierra never changed—and that's why she loved him.

Yvonne came up and leaned on the white paddock fence. "He's full of himself."

Samantha nodded and looked around, taking in the scent of the famous Kentucky bluegrass and inhaling the warm Kentucky air. A slight breeze ruffled her red ponytail. "So, ready for a trail ride?" she asked.

Yvonne's dark, almond-shaped eyes sparkled. "You bet!" she said. She stretched her hand up to Sierra's glossy mane and stood still while he snuffled by her ear.

A few minutes later the two young women had saddled up, and they started down the grassy lanes between the paddocks, heading for the main pasture trail that circled Whitebrook. Samantha was riding Shining, and as always she felt a thrill at the fact that the gorgeous Thoroughbred belonged to her.

"Hey, guess what?" Yvonne said as she rode Sierra alongside Shining. "There's a new horse in training at Tor's stable."

"Oh, yeah?" Samantha asked, interested.

"The owner's name is Angelique Dubret. The horse is a big Dutch warmblood named Appraiser. You should see him. He's tall and well muscled, with a beautiful head and big, flat knees. Boy, can he jump!"

Samantha smiled. "Well, Angelique's come to the right place. Tor really knows how to make the most out of talented jumpers. I wonder why he didn't tell me about Appraiser. Has Angelique shown much?"

Yvonne nodded. "I guess she's been on the show circuit for a while, and she's won a few trophies here and there, but now she really wants to get into the higher levels. She's a gutsy rider, and she'll try anything." Yvonne leaned forward and patted Sierra's neck. "Anyway, next time you're at Tor's, you should check him out."

"I will," Samantha said. "Hey, Sierra really seems to be behaving himself today. You're riding him well."

Yvonne grinned. "Thanks."

Samantha gave Shining more rein. The filly dropped her head, stretched her neck, and lengthened her stride as she relaxed. Samantha was reminded that not long ago she never could have given the filly her head on the trail. Shining had been abused as a youngster. She'd imagined that a terror hid behind every bush on the trail, and she'd shied violently at everything. Now, however, she trusted

Samantha completely. She was certainly a different horse these days.

The horses made their way up the trail and stopped at the crest of a hill. From this vantage point Samantha could see the entire farm spread out below her. White rail fences surrounded the grounds, encircling the various barns, which were kept in meticulous repair and painted the traditional brick-red color. A few horses grazed in the paddocks, but the training oval was empty. Come sunup tomorrow, however, the oval would be bustling with activity. Samantha's eyes traveled to the farmhouse where Ashleigh and Mike lived with Mike's father, then to the small cottage beside it where she lived.

She inhaled deeply. How she loved living on a breeding and training farm, surrounded by the horses she loved so much. Yes, she decided, she was lucky, and there was so much to look forward to right now. She clucked softly and gave Shining a slight nudge with her heels. The filly set out at a smart trot, her hooves crunching in the sweet-smelling pine needles, and the two quickly caught up with Sierra and Yvonne.

After they'd trotted briskly for a while, they slowed and let the horses enjoy a leisurely walk. "So, have you made any decisions about when you're going to race Shining again?" Yvonne asked.

Samantha rubbed the tip of her slightly freckled

nose with her riding glove and nodded. "I've been thinking about entering her in a race at Churchill Downs sometime in late June."

"Great," said Yvonne happily. "I know she'll do as brilliantly as she did at Keeneland."

"She's right, you know. You are brilliant," Samantha said to Shining, patting her horse lovingly. She turned to Yvonne. "I'd like to race her sooner than that, but with all the things coming up—the prom, graduation, the parties and all—I really won't have that much time to work her. And I want to be sure she's absolutely ready before she sets one hoof on the track."

"I don't blame you," Yvonne said, nodding her dark head. "By the way, I heard Lavinia Townsend's new filly won a race at Churchill Downs last week."

Samantha's face darkened as she thought about Lavinia Townsend. The spoiled, wealthy woman had married the son of the owner of Townsend Acres and had been causing trouble for Ashleigh and Samantha for years. One of her most recent exploits had almost cost Wonder's filly, Townsend Princess, her racing career. Lavinia had taken the filly out on the track, and because of Lavinia's inexperience, Princess had bolted and fallen, fracturing her leg. Lavinia had shown no remorse, and she'd blamed the entire thing on the filly.

"Yeah, I got to hear all about it," she said. "Lavinia

11

and Brad were here the next day with Mr. Townsend, and Lavinia couldn't stop gloating. She's the biggest pain. I think they came over just to brag, but they also kept looking at Shining. Of course, Lavinia came up with her usual negative comments, but I'm not going to let her bother me. I can't stand to look at her ever since she hurt Princess."

Yvonne frowned. "How is Princess, anyway?" she asked.

"I heard she's doing great. The vet X-rayed her leg, and he says it looks good. Ashleigh and Mr. Townsend are going to talk with Ken Maddock this week about putting her back in training again."

"Hey, that's great!" Yvonne exclaimed. "Ashleigh must be thrilled."

"Oh, she is," Samantha said. "Of course, she'd be even more thrilled if Lavinia would never set foot on Whitebrook property again."

"That would be too much to hope for," Yvonne said, shaking her head.

After their ride the girls dismounted, ran the stirrup irons up the leathers, and loosened the girths on the saddles. They untacked the horses, then put on their personalized leather halters. Samantha took a bucket of lukewarm water and gently sponged Shining's glistening chest and girth area. She ran the sponge behind the filly's ears and under her throat. When she was finished, she took a stiff dandy brush and ran it in a circular motion over Shining's coat. She then followed up with a soft body brush, finishing her meticulous grooming with a thorough cleaning of Shining's well-shaped hooves. Yvonne went through the same routine with Sierra.

Once the horses were sheeted and back in their stalls, Samantha drove Yvonne home. When she got back to the farm, she went up to the cottage to make dinner for herself and her dad. After dinner she'd have to spend a few hours studying for finals.

It was late when Samantha went back to the barn to look in on the horses one last time before going to bed. It was a moonlit night, and she found the latch easily and slipped inside. As she walked down the aisle she could hear the rustling of straw as a horse shifted position. It seemed so quiet and peaceful in the barn that Samantha was surprised to see Shining was awake and alert when she approached her box stall. Shining's ears were pricked, and she looked nervously toward the stall next to her. She snorted and pawed her bedding, tossing her head anxiously. Samantha froze. Something must be wrong with one of the orphan foals!

She hurried over to the foals' stall and looked in. The two little foals were curled up in the straw next to each other, but they were awake and testing the air curiously with their nostrils. Nothing wrong there.

"Hey, li'l guys," Samantha said softly. "How come

13

you're awake?" And what was Shining so nervous about? Samantha wondered as she looked around the darkened stall. In the dim light, her eye caught a dark shape nestled in the corner on a pile of bedding. Curious, Samantha let herself into the stall and moved cautiously toward the bundle. It was a blond-haired girl dressed in jeans and a light jacket. She looked no more than ten or eleven years old. She was sound asleep, halfcovered by an old horse blanket, her arm flung across the straw.

Samantha stared at the girl and sucked in her breath. Who was she, and what on earth was she doing sleeping in a stall at Whitebrook?

GINGERLY SAMANTHA STEPPED OVER TO THE GIRL AND LAID a gentle hand on her shoulder.

The girl's eyes flew open and she sat up, throwing back the blanket. The foals started, but they didn't move. They, like Samantha, continued staring wide-eyed at the stranger.

"Don't worry. I'm leaving," the girl said defensively, brushing her tangled hair out of her face as she stood up. "Just give me a sec."

Samantha stepped back. "No, you don't have to do that," she said, trying to think. "Just tell me why you're here."

"It's warm in here," the girl said. "And these little guys looked . . . lonely."

She looked down at her battered sneakers and shrugged, a scowl on her face. She yawned, and

Samantha could see that she was exhausted.

"What's your name?"

"Cindy, and I wasn't hurting anyone. I just needed a place to sleep, and it seemed safe."

"But where do you live?" Samantha asked. "Your parents must be frantic wondering where you are."

"I don't live anywhere," the girl said. Then she added: "And my parents aren't frantic. They're dead."

Samantha tried not to let her shock register on her face. She was exhausted too. This was no time to ask twenty questions. She'd ask the girl to come up to the cottage to sleep for the night, and figure out what to do in the morning.

"Tell you what," Samantha said. "Why don't you come home with me? It will certainly be a more comfortable place to spend the night, and then we can sort out everything else in the morning."

The girl jutted out her chin and shook her head. "I'd rather stay here," she said, looking over at the foals.

Samantha finally persuaded her to come, and after a couple of minutes she led Cindy up to the cottage. She got her settled on the couch with several blankets before wearily climbing into bed herself, her mind spinning with the events of the evening. She'd have to make sure she got up before her dad in the morning. She didn't want him finding Cindy before she'd had a chance to explain what had happened.

The next morning Samantha awoke with a start as she remembered Whitebrook's strange guest. She showered and threw on her clothes, then made her way down to the living room. Cindy was just awakening, her eyes blinking in the dim light of the unfamiliar surroundings.

"Good morning," Samantha said.

"It's still dark," the girl pointed out.

Samantha smiled. "I know. But we get up early here. There are a lot of horses who are already up, nickering to be fed, and we do all the workouts first thing in the morning."

Cindy clambered off the couch, and Samantha looked at her rumpled clothes.

"I'll be right back," she said. She ran up to her room and found a shirt and jeans she'd outgrown in the bottom of a drawer. "Here. I'll show you where the bathroom is and you can freshen up and change. Then we'll have breakfast and we can talk."

Cindy shook her head. "These clothes are fine." Samantha was about to try again when her dad came into the kitchen. He looked at Cindy, and his eyes widened in surprise. He gave Samantha a questioning look.

"Dad, this is Cindy," Samantha said. "She was— she was asleep in the orphans' stall last night, and I told her it would be more comfortable here."

"What was she doing in the orphans' stall? Aren't her par—"

Samantha quickly cut him off with a shake of her head. He poured his coffee and studied the girl. "Well, how about some breakfast?"

"I'm not hungry."

Samantha glanced at Cindy, then at her dad. She poured some cereal in two bowls, then set out some fruit. Cindy looked at the food.

"Go ahead," Samantha said.

Cindy dropped onto a chair, then attacked the food like a wild animal who hadn't eaten for days.

"Where are you from?" Mr. McLean asked, draining the last of his coffee.

Cindy poured another bowlful of cereal. "A home," she mumbled. "Foster home in town. I ran away." She glared in a challenging way at Samantha and her dad, then went on. "They're mean to me there. I hate the Hadleys. I told them so, and then I took off. You gonna turn me in?"

Mr. McLean regarded her steadily. "Turn you in? Hadn't crossed my mind. We've got a lot of horses who need some attention this morning. Let's go down there and get to work, and we'll figure out your situation afterward."

Cindy looked relieved. She pushed back her bowl.

"Do you know much about horses?" Samantha asked as they walked toward the mares' barn.

"The Hadleys have horses. They make us foster kids take care of them—groom them, muck stalls." Her face tightened. "They never let us ride them, though. We just do all the grunt work."

"That's too bad," Samantha said sympathetically. "Sounds like you would have liked to ride."

Cindy shrugged. "I guess, but I knew it would never happen, so I didn't let myself think about it."

Samantha called to the groom, who was measuring some additives into a bucket for one of the broodmares. "Good morning, Vic. This is Cindy."

Cindy looked at the groom but remained silent.

"That's Vic Taleski," Samantha explained as she led the way to Shining's stall. "You don't have to be afraid of him."

"I'm not afraid."

"He's one of the grooms here at Whitebrook. And this is Shining. She's my horse. That kitten sitting on her back is Flurry, one of the barn cats."

Cindy's eyes grew round with awe as she took in the magnificent horse standing before her. "She's beautiful," she said softly.

Shining whickered throatily, and Samantha smiled. "Thank you. I think so too."

She slipped inside the stall and set Flurry out in the aisle.

"Cats and horses get along well, don't they?" Cindy remarked, leaning down to pet Flurry.

19

Samantha nodded. "All of our barn cats have a favorite horse."

Cindy leaned up against the stall to get a closer look at Shining. "She's named Shining because she's so shiny, right?"

"Sort of. But Shining didn't always look like this," Samantha said with barely concealed pride. "When she first came here, she had been neglected and abused, and it showed."

She looked at Cindy and found herself thinking, *Just like you. Neglected and abused—and just as distrustful.*

Both girls turned when they heard footsteps coming down the barn aisle. Ashleigh appeared at Shining's stall. "Morning, Sammy. Well, hello," she said in surprise when she saw Cindy.

"Ashleigh, this is Cindy," Samantha said. "Ashleigh's a jockey and trainer. Cindy's staying at our cottage."

Ashleigh gave Samantha a questioning look, but Samantha didn't want to go into a long explanation now. Careful that Cindy didn't see, she mouthed the word "Later." Ashleigh nodded. "Nice to meet you," she said to Cindy. "I'm on my way to visit Wonder. See you in a bit."

"Ashleigh's a good friend, and one of the owners of this farm," Samantha explained to Cindy as they stepped out of Shining's stall. She led the girl over to the orphans' stall, where Len was feeding them from two big bottles.

He glanced up when he heard them approach. "Morning," he said. "These little guys are hungry this morning."

"Len, I'd like you to meet Cindy. This is Len, the stable manager. Cindy was our guest last night. Can you use a hand, Len?" she asked, with a burst of inspiration.

Len nodded and waved Cindy in. "Sure could. These youngsters get pushier every day."

"Really, I can feed them?"

Samantha nodded, and was gratified to see a fleeting smile cross Cindy's face. She watched for a few moments as Len showed Cindy how to hold the bottle and gave her instructions in his calm, reassuring voice. Samantha walked on to the training barn, satisfied that Cindy was in good hands.

Samantha's father stepped out of one of the stalls, where he'd been taking off some leg wraps. His eyes twinkled as he said, "Well, that was some surprise."

Samantha cracked a grin. "You're not kidding."

"Did you manage to find out anything about her? If she's a runaway, we'll have to call the youth authorities, learn what the story is. Maybe they'll find a new home for her."

"I hope so," Samantha said. "She certainly shouldn't have to go back to the house she ran away from. But

Dad, please, let's wait and see if we can get the whole story from Cindy before you make any calls."

Samantha's father thought this over, then slowly shook his head. "I know it doesn't seem right, sweetie. But we have to do it. Someone must be looking for her. We have to let them know she's okay."

Samantha reluctantly nodded. "I'm sure they're worried."

"Well, there's work to do. As soon as I'm done in here I'll make the call from the office."

Samantha watched her father disappear down the aisle, then went back to the cottage to get ready for school.

Once she was in class, it was nearly impossible for her to concentrate. She couldn't stop thinking about Cindy. At lunchtime she told Yvonne and Maureen about finding the young girl in the barn.

"You're kidding!" Yvonne's eyes widened. "What's going to happen to her?"

"I don't know," Samantha said. "Guess I'll find out when I get home. My dad was going to let the authorities know Cindy is with us."

As soon as she got home that afternoon she headed straight for the barns. She didn't see Cindy, but she spotted her father standing by a paddock, watching Rocky Heights, a young horse that Mike had bought at the auction where he'd bought Shining.

"I called the child protection agency," Samantha's dad explained when he saw Samantha. "Seems they have a file on Cindy—that is her name, Cindy Blake—this thick." He held up his thumb and forefinger, spreading them about three inches apart. "She's run away from several homes. They're checking with her latest foster home, then getting back to me. Apparently the people at the home hadn't even reported her missing yet."

"So what are we going to do?" Samantha asked, watching the colt. The big gray was snorting and bucking playfully in the sunshine.

Samantha and her father walked on to the paddock where some of the mares and older foals were turned out. Len was inside, adjusting the creep, an area with a low bar that the foals could slip under to get to a special feed trough that the mares couldn't reach. Cindy was behind Len, patting the foals. She seemed completely at ease with the animals, and they didn't seem to mind her unfamiliar touch. Samantha noticed how Cindy's small shoulder blades stuck out through the back of her shirt.

"I feel so sorry for her," she whispered to her father. "She seems like a . . . a lost foal or something."

Samantha's father nodded. "Well, we'll figure out something. In the meantime, let's be kind to her and show her the world isn't always a terrible place. It must seem that way to her right now."

Samantha left her father and went to look in on Shining. Then she poked her head into the orphan foals' stall, happy to see that Cindy was there, eagerly watching Len as he got ready to feed the small horses.

Samantha regarded her for a moment, taking in every detail of her appearance, from the thin, worn cotton shirt to the dirty sneakers with holes in the toes. Her hair was tangled and stringy and fell forward over her face. Once again Samantha was reminded of when Shining had arrived at Whitebrook, her coat scraggly, her mane tangled, and her bones jutting through her flesh.

"Hi, Cindy," Samantha said. "How's it going? Getting ready to feed the foals again? Maybe that can be your job while you're here, if it's okay with Len, that is."

"Sounds great to me," Len responded. He handed Cindy one of the bottles. Cindy's eyes softened as she fed the foal and gently stroked its nose. She was certainly more at ease with horses than with people. Samantha had a feeling it wasn't going to be easy to break through Cindy's wall of distrust.

At dinner Cindy wolfed down her food silently, never taking her eyes from her plate. When Samantha was finished, she realized that in all the commotion caused by Cindy's arrival, she'd forgotten that she and Tor were going to the movies. She called him and told him briefly about the recent events so that he'd be prepared when he met Cindy.

Samantha was brushing her hair when she heard the crunch of gravel outside and knew it must be Tor. She grabbed a sweater and ran to the front door. Tor was walking up the stone walkway. He pushed back a lock of blond hair and grinned at her, revealing his straight white teeth.

"Come in for a minute," Samantha said after she and Tor exchanged a soft kiss.

"Where's Cindy?" he asked.

"She went down to the barn just after dinner. She can't seem to get enough of the horses. I'll introduce you later." Samantha led him to the kitchen, where her dad and Beth Raines, the woman he was dating, were loading the last of the supper dishes into the dishwasher.

When Mr. McLean saw Tor, he dried his hands on a dish towel and reached out to shake hands.

Beth too greeted him warmly. "I hear that the Pony Commandos are doing great," she said, referring to the group of six disabled children that Tor and Samantha were teaching to ride. "Janet was telling me that the children have been enjoying themselves so much," Beth went on. Janet Roarsh was her partner in her aerobics studio. "You two are doing a fantastic job."

Samantha smiled at the compliment and found

herself thinking about how comfortable she felt with Beth these days. It hadn't always been that way. Samantha's mother had been killed in a riding accident almost six years ago, and when her dad had first started dating Beth, Samantha hadn't been thrilled. An aerobics instructor in Lexington, Beth didn't know the least thing about horses. Samantha had been cool toward the woman for quite a while, and it hadn't done her relationship with her father any good. Somewhere along the way, however, she and Beth had forged an understanding. Now Samantha could honestly say that she'd grown fond of Beth.

When the conversation died down, Samantha slipped her hand into Tor's.

"I know we could talk all night," she said. "But it would be nice to catch the first part of the movie so we know what's going on."

"You two head out," Samantha's father said. "Have a good time."

Moments later Samantha and Tor were breezing along the road toward Lexington. Dusk was settling, and a few stars were twinkling in the night sky. Samantha looked out the window for a moment.

"Nice night," Tor said, glancing upward.

"Umm-hmm," Samantha agreed, reaching over to massage Tor's shoulder. "Hey, I had an idea yesterday."

"Uh-huh. About what?"

"I thought I would have a pre-prom dinner party for you, me, Yvonne and Gregg, and Maureen and her date," she said.

"Sounds good to me. And now I have an idea for you. I was thinking that we should plan a summer show for the Pony Commandos," he said. "We'll have a couple of different classes, and there'll be special ribbons for everyone."

Samantha's face broke into a delighted grin. "Tor, that's a great idea. They'll be so excited! Wait till we tell Mandy." Her face softened as she thought of how excited the little girl would be.

The Pony Commandos were really doing great. Many of them had limited use of their legs and had been in physical therapy for months, but hadn't started to improve until they'd started riding. All the children looked forward to their riding lessons and had developed special relationships with the horses. Especially Mandy Jarvis. She had probably made the most progress, and had particularly taken to Shining. In fact, Samantha had come close to selling her beloved horse to Mandy's parents, but in the end they had decided that a smaller horse would be better for the little girl. They'd bought a pony named Butterball from Tor's stable instead. Mandy loved Butterball, but she was never happier than when she was watching Shining race or being around her at Whitebrook.

"You know, Mandy's got her heart set on serious jumping someday," she said thoughtfully. "Do you think she'll ever be able to?"

Tor paused and considered it for a moment, a slight frown crossing his handsome face. "I don't know," he said softly. "Maybe, if she keeps improving the way she has been." He sat up a little straighter. "Then again, I don't know anyone with more guts than Mandy."

"She sure is determined," Samantha agreed.

"You know, I was planning to come over tomorrow afternoon and give Sierra a training session," Tor said. "Maybe Mandy would like to watch."

Samantha nodded. "No maybe about it. Mandy would love it."

The rest of the ride to the theater they discussed their plans for Sierra, and then Tor told her about the shows he wanted to compete in during the summer. Top Hat, his white Thoroughbred jumper, was training well, and Tor was looking forward to the Virginia show he and Top Hat would be competing in toward the end of July.

After the movie they headed straight back to White-brook because it was a school night. Tor walked Samantha up to the front door and gave her a warm kiss. As she headed toward her room she could hear Tor's truck roar off into the night. She slipped downstairs to get a glass of water, and in the dim light she could see Cindy sitting up on the couch, hugging her knees.

"Hi, Cindy," Samantha said softly. "Everything okay?"

The girl turned her head. She was silent.

Samantha tried again. "It's okay," she said softly. "You can talk to me."

The girl regarded her with wary eyes, as if trying to decide if she could trust her. Finally she spoke. "The Child Protection Services people called back tonight," she said. "The Hadleys—those are the people I lived with—wanted to come get me right away, but your dad talked them out of it."

"That's good!" Samantha exclaimed.

The girl shook her head. "Yeah, but I know them. They'll try to take me away. It's not 'cause they want me, either. They just like the money the state gives them."

Samantha's heart went out to the girl. "Something will work out. You'll see," she said uncertainly.

As Samantha went to her room, however, she wondered if she should have said that. She didn't know how these things worked. Maybe the Hadleys could just come and get Cindy anytime they wanted, and there wouldn't be anything anyone could do about it. If that happened, Samantha was certain Cindy would never trust anyone again. She had to think of a way to help her.

3

AS SOON AS SAMANTHA ARRIVED HOME FROM SCHOOL THE next day, she hurriedly changed into her work clothes and headed for the stables. She caught a glimpse of Cindy leaning on the rail of one of the paddocks. Samantha looked in on Shining and Wonder, petted their velvety muzzles for a few moments, then headed over to Cindy.

"Hi," she said.

"Hello."

"How are the orphans?" Samantha asked.

"Okay."

"A friend of mine is going to jump one of the horses in a little while. He's a steeplechaser. Come watch if you want."

"Okay," Cindy said, a flicker of interest in her eyes. She followed Samantha over to the barn where Vic had Sierra in crossties and was grooming him. Tor was already there, dressed in riding gear and adjusting Sierra's bridle. He smiled at Samantha, who introduced him to Cindy.

"Nice to meet you," he said. "Are you a steeplechasing fan?"

"I don't know. I've never seen a steeplechase."

"Well, you're about to," Tor said. "It's pretty exciting. Mandy will be here any minute. I'll take a few minutes to warm up, then we'll put Sierra at the hurdles and let him show his stuff."

"Who's Mandy?" Cindy asked Samantha.

"She's one of our Pony Commandos," Samantha explained. She told Cindy about the six disabled children who took riding lessons at the Nelsons' stable. "I think you'll really like her."

Just as Tor and Sierra set off for the turf course where the practice hurdles were set up, Mrs. Jarvis's car pulled up to the farm. Samantha hurried over to greet Mandy and her mom. She stood by as the little girl maneuvered herself out of the car, struggling with the heavy metal braces on her legs.

"Hi, Samantha!" Mandy cried, her coffee-colored eyes gleaming with excitement. "Have they started? Did we miss anything?"

Mrs. Jarvis smiled fondly at her daughter. "We got stuck in traffic, and Mandy was beside herself. She was sure she was going to miss out on something."

Samantha ruffled the little girl's curly hair. "You didn't miss a thing. Tor's just warming up Sierra now. He'll be ready to jump in a few minutes. I'd like you to meet Cindy—she's staying with us at White-brook."

"Hi," Mandy said, taking Cindy's hand as they all set off toward the turf course. Cindy trailed along while Mandy chattered nonstop. "Do you like horses as much as I do? Do you want to jump? I do. Course, steeplechasing's a lot different than jumping, but I can still learn something by watching Tor ride Sierra, so when I start to jump higher, I'll know what to do."

Samantha and Mrs. Jarvis exchanged looks. Soon they were at the edge of the turf course. Tor was cantering Sierra, collecting him and balancing him. After a while he gave the liver chestnut more rein, moved him in closer to the center of the track, and urged him toward the first hedgelike hurdle. The horse stretched out his neck and lengthened his stride.

"Sierra looks good today," Samantha commented.

"He *is* doing good, isn't he?" Mandy said excitedly as Sierra cleared the hurdle with room to spare.

Samantha nodded. "Tor's letting him find his own distances today. Sierra has more experience now and can judge his takeoff points pretty well."

"Isn't Tor scared to jump so high and so fast?" Cindy asked breathlessly.

"He knows what he's doing," Samantha said.

They watched as Tor put Sierra over jump after jump. The big horse was eager and cleared every hurdle smoothly. Finally Tor pulled him up and walked over to the group.

Samantha patted Sierra's neck, now dark with sweat. "Well done, big guy," she said to the horse.

Sierra whoofed appreciatively and stretched his nose out to where Mandy's little hand was reaching to pat him, too.

"So what did you think, girls?" Tor asked, sliding off Sierra's back and loosening the girth on his saddle.

Mandy clapped her hands. "He was wonderful. The best. He's going to win lots more races, isn't he?"

Tor took off his helmet and pushed back his hair. "That's the idea," he said with a chuckle. He replaced his helmet and brought the reins over Sierra's head. "We'd better walk him out and cool him down. I'll see you back at the barn."

Mandy watched Tor and Sierra head off and sighed deeply. "Tor knows so much about jumping." She turned toward Samantha. "If only I could ride like that someday."

Once again, Samantha's eyes and Mrs. Jarvis's connected over the top of Mandy's head. Samantha's mind raced as she tried to think of what to say.

"Well, Mandy, if anyone has the guts to try, you do. You've been doing so well in your jumping classes. And guess what? Tor and I are planning another show for the Pony Commandos this summer."

Mandy grinned with excitement. "That will give me and Butterball something to practice for. Hooray!"

After Mandy and Tor had gone, Samantha helped with the evening chores. When all the horses had been fed and bedded down for the night, she headed toward Shining's stall. As she approached she saw something she could hardly believe. Cindy was sitting up on Shining's back! Moving slowly so as not to startle Shining, Samantha went to the stall door.

"Cindy, what are you doing? You should never get on a horse's back in a stall," Samantha said sternly. "Do you realize what could happen if Shining were to spook with you up there? You and the horse could really get hurt!"

A series of expressions darted across Cindy's face, but she didn't reply. She jumped down, threw open the stall door, and brushed past Samantha, then bolted down the aisle into the dusk.

"Cindy, wait!" Samantha shouted, but she was already gone. Too late, Samantha realized how her sharp words must have sounded to Cindy, who had probably heard sharp words all too often. Things with Cindy certainly weren't going the way Samantha had hoped.

A few minutes later Samantha found Cindy sitting

by the cottage steps, staring stonily at the ground.

"I'm sorry, I didn't mean to be short with you," Samantha said. "It's just that I was scared."

Cindy wiped her face with her dirty sleeve. "I used to sit on the farm horses' backs in their shed all the time at the Hadleys' farm," she mumbled.

"Well, it doesn't really matter what you did there. Farm horses are different from racehorses. Racehorses are bred to be very sensitive and alert. Shining's as gentle as they come, but she still could have been startled. So please don't do that again."

Cindy nodded.

"Come on. Let's go eat. I don't know about you, but I'm starving."

The next day after school Samantha changed and hurried to the mares' barn. Cindy was leaning idly against the stall bars, watching Shining.

"Hi," Samantha said.

Cindy mumbled a reply.

"I'm going to groom Shining." Samantha held up a dandy brush. "Would you like to watch?"

She didn't wait for an answer but let herself into Shining's stall. Shining whuffed into Samantha's palm, and Samantha led her out to the crossties. Cindy followed and reached up to pat Shining on her muzzle. She pulled her hand back and giggled.

"Her whiskers tickle, don't they?" Samantha said,

setting down the brush and selecting a hoofpick.

Cindy bent over the grooming box and studied the tools for a moment, then stood up again and watched as Samantha carefully started cleaning one of Shining's hooves.

"Doesn't that hurt?" Cindy asked.

Samantha shook her head. "The hoof is like a big, hard fingernail. This part—called the frog—is a little more sensitive," she explained, pointing to some V-shaped tissue on the underside of the hoof. Cindy moved in closer and touched the area. "It acts as a sort of shock absorber."

"You know everything about horses, don't you?" Cindy said matter-of-factly.

Samantha smiled and gently set down Shining's foot. "Oh, I know lots of people who know more," she said. "Here." She handed the hoofpick to Cindy. "Why don't you try the next foot? Go up to Shining's shoulder and gently lean against it, then run your hand down her leg to let her know that you want her to pick up her foot."

Cindy studied the hoofpick in her hand, then took a deep breath. She walked to Shining's right foreleg and, following Samantha's instructions, ran her hand downward, picked up the hoof, and carefully cleaned it out as she had seen Samantha do. When she set it back down, she smiled shyly.

"You're a natural," Samantha said.

"Thanks." Cindy looked proud.

"So what did you think of our steeplechaser yesterday?" Samantha asked.

"He's a beautiful horse, and so playful. I liked him. I liked Mandy too. She loves horses as much as I do."

Samantha nodded, encouraging the girl to keep talking.

"I used to pretend that the Hadleys' horses were mine. They weren't pretty like Shining or Sierra, but I talked to them. I'd go hide in the shed with them when the Hadleys got mad at me."

"Were there other foster kids in the home, too?" Samantha asked.

"Yeah. Three others. The more kids, the more money for the Hadleys."

Samantha waited to hear more, but Cindy didn't go on. Samantha decided not to press it any further, and she spent the rest of the afternoon letting Cindy help her groom and bathe the horses, amazed at how at ease Cindy was with the animals and the task.

During dinner Beth asked Cindy about her foster home. Cindy answered in monosyllables in between big helpings of fried chicken and steamed vegetables. She didn't seem willing to reveal anything. After dinner she went back down to the barn to help Len feed the orphans. When she was gone, Beth turned to Samantha and her dad.

"You're really going to have to make some decisions

about what to do with Cindy. She needs some routine and order in her life. It can't be good running from one situation into another the way she has."

Mr. McLean nodded. "I made a few more phone calls today. The Hadleys want her to come back. Mrs. Lovell—that's Cindy's caseworker—said that she'll have to go. I told Mrs. Lovell that we want to keep her, and that I felt they ought to investigate the Hadley place, considering how poorly Cindy says she was treated."

"Oh, Dad, that's a great idea. She really likes it here," Samantha said. "Do you think she'll be able to stay with us?"

"Well, like I said, the Hadleys want her back," Samantha's father said quietly. "Mrs. Lovell says it's best for her to be with her foster parents."

"But the Hadleys want her just because they want the money," Samantha protested. "Cindy told me."

Beth got up to make herself a cup of herbal tea. "Ian, why don't we go downtown together tomorrow to speak to the authorities? There are only a couple of weeks of school left, so maybe they'll let her skip the rest while we figure out what to do." Beth sipped her tea thoughtfully. "It would be a shame if she had to go back to a place where she wasn't really wanted."

The next afternoon when Samantha returned from school, she saw Beth's car in the driveway. When she entered the kitchen, Beth was setting a sandwich on the table for Cindy.

"Can I eat this at the stable?" Cindy asked.

Beth smiled. "Go on," she said. Cindy grabbed her sandwich and bolted out the back door.

"Your father and I took Cindy downtown," she said wearily. "We just got back. What a lot of red tape."

Samantha took an orange from the fruit basket and started peeling it. "What happened? Can she stay?"

"For now," Beth said. "Your dad did a lot of talking to convince the people in charge that Whitebrook was a good place for Cindy."

"She's really had a tough life," Samantha said, popping an orange section into her mouth.

Beth nodded. "I don't think we know the half of it. The Hadleys sound awful. They have several horses, and it seems they make the foster kids do most of the work. Cindy's the only one who actually ran away, though. But when we asked her to tell Mrs. Lovell about how she was treated, she just clammed up. Unless she tells her what went on there, I have a feeling Cindy will be returned to the Hadleys eventually. Mrs. Lovell agreed to let her stay here temporarily while her case is being checked, but she didn't seem thrilled by the fact that your dad is a single parent. It's clear that the agency favors two-parent homes."

"I don't see how there can be any question about

my dad," Samantha protested. "Anyway, I still don't see how they can consider sending her back to a place where she was so unhappy."

"These things work in strange ways," Beth said. "But we can't give up. Maybe we can figure something out."

Samantha was up before dawn the next morning so she could get in a couple of workouts before heading off to school. She took one of the fillies for a slow gallop around the oval, savoring the feeling of the cool morning air whipping at her face. "We'll just take it easy today, girl," Samantha said as the filly fought for her head. When Samantha was finished, she hurried to take the reins of one of Mike's two-year-olds. She would be breezing him through four furlongs to sharpen him up for his first race.

"I want to see this one open up," Mike instructed her. Samantha pushed her goggles down and nodded, her attention on the big bay colt she'd just mounted. When the workout was over, she turned the horse over to Vic, then hurried to Shining's stall to clean out her bedding.

"Good morning, girl," Samantha said, rubbing her filly's mane.

Shining whuffed loudly and Samantha started pitching forkfuls of straw into the wheelbarrow, then paused for a moment, leaning on the pitchfork and letting her glance rest on Shining's glossy roan quarters. Shining nuzzled her under her arm, then nibbled her way upward, where she whoofed sweet breath in Samantha's ear.

Samantha reached up to scratch her behind the ears. "You are beautiful, you know," she whispered. She ran her fingers through Shining's mane, which cascaded silkily against her neck. "And I have big plans for you. Tomorrow morning we'll put in a light workout, okay?"

"Sammy, you in there?" Ashleigh's clear voice rang down the barn aisle.

Her dark head appeared over the stall partition. "I thought I'd find you here."

"What's up?" Samantha asked.

Ashleigh smiled broadly. "Guess what? Ken Maddock says Princess is ready to go back into training again. She's totally, one hundred percent better."

Samantha whooped loudly. "All right!"

Shining, sensing the excitement, snorted vigorously.

Ashleigh grew more serious. "Maddock agrees that we'll have to take it slow, but if she trains well, she could be ready to race by fall, maybe even late summer."

"Way to go," Samantha said. "Lavinia had better stay away from her!"

"Don't worry," Ashleigh said forcefully. "Mr. Townsend and Maddock won't let her anywhere near Princess."

Cindy's blond head appeared outside the stall. She was wearing stiff new jeans that hung on her thin frame and a crisp yellow blouse. Her sneakers were new, and her hair was pulled into a lopsided ponytail. Samantha knew Beth had taken Cindy shopping the day before. She didn't exactly look happy about her new clothes.

"Good morning, Shining," she said, her eyes lighting up. It was amazing how she seemed to be a different person when she was with the horses. She reached out to stroke the filly's nose, then dropped a soft kiss on the end of it. "Well, I'm off to help Len with the orphans. See you later."

"She seems much happier than when she first arrived," Ashleigh commented once Cindy was gone.

Samantha nodded. "I know. She really loves the horses, especially the orphans and Shining." She quickly explained to Ashleigh what Beth had told her the day before about Cindy staying with them temporarily.

"That's great. I'm not surprised she's so attached to the new foals," Ashleigh said softly. "She must know just how they feel."

"She's really a natural with the horses. Len loves having her around, and so do the grooms and exercise riders. She's incredibly eager to learn and be helpful."

Ashleigh laughed. "Sounds a lot like us when we were her age."

Early the next morning, as Samantha tacked up Shining for her workout, she saw Mr. Townsend, Lavinia, and Brad walking down the barn aisle. Samantha groaned as she set the light racing saddle on Shining's back. The last people she wanted to see today were snooty Lavinia and her husband, Brad.

"Good morning," Clay Townsend said as they approached.

Samantha bid her good mornings politely and turned to give Shining's girth a final adjustment.

"We're just here looking things over," Lavinia said haughtily. She yawned pointedly, as if the goings-on at Whitebrook bored her. But Samantha wasn't fooled. She knew that Lavinia was only covering up her interest in seeing how the Whitebrook stock were training.

She made no comment as she and Shining started down the barn aisle. She felt her shoulders tense as she realized that the three were following her over to the training oval. "Great," she muttered to herself. She took Shining over to the rail where Ashleigh was standing, stopwatch in her hand, watching as Blues King, who'd won the previous year's Breeders' Cup Sprint, took his gallop around the track.

"Hi, Samantha. Shining's next, after Rocky Heights," Ashleigh said, smiling over at Samantha.

"Blues King looks sharp today," Samantha said, trying not to let the fact that the Townsends were there get to her as she watched the exercise rider jump off King and get into Rocky's saddle. Oh, why wouldn't Lavinia go away so she could work with her horse in peace?

Mr. Townsend turned to Ashleigh. "We're going to have to talk about Pride's stud book for next year," he said. "We've had more applicants than I'd imagined. We'll have to be selective about the mares we breed him to."

Ashleigh beamed. "Well, that's the kind of problem we like to have. That's wonderful!"

Samantha looked to see if Lavinia had heard and noticed that Lavinia and Brad were critically studying Shining.

"Well, she looks better than when she was dragged in here," Lavinia said loudly to Brad. "But winning that race was definitely a fluke. She really doesn't have what it takes to be a steady winner like Her Majesty."

"Oh, I don't know about that," Ashleigh told them.

Samantha's eyes flashed as Ashleigh gave her a leg up. She pressed her helmet firmly on her head and checked Shining's girth one final time. "We'll show her!" Samantha hissed to Shining. Shining's sensitive ears swiveled back to listen. "She hardly knows the front end of a horse from the back."

Samantha suddenly narrowed her eyes. "Forget what I said yesterday about a light workout. Let's make Lavinia eat her words. We'll give her something to worry about. Let's breeze out the last quarter—show them your stuff. Wait a sec, Ashleigh," Samantha said. "Change of plans. Shining and I are going to go for it. Clock us for the last quarter."

Ashleigh gave her a knowing glance and smiled.

Samantha headed Shining onto the track and urged the filly into a trot, then a canter.

"She's got a long way to go to be in the same class as Her Majesty," Samantha heard Lavinia say as they passed by.

Samantha gritted her teeth and leaned forward, giving Shining her head. Shining jumped forward eagerly, lengthening her stride and opening up at a moderate gallop. Samantha could feel the wind slapping at her face and could hear the rhythmic pounding of Shining's hooves as her ground-eating stride propelled them around the track for the first three-quarters of a mile.

As they approached the quarter pole, Samantha clucked and let the filly out into a breezing gallop. Shining shifted gears, and they started flying down the track. They swept around the far turn toward the wire, Shining putting every ounce of heart into the gallop. "Good girl," Samantha crooned as they passed the mile pole. She stood in her stirrups and pulled Shining back into a canter. Samantha glanced over to Ashleigh and wasn't surprised to see her flash a thumbs-up.

"Twenty-three for the last quarter!" Ashleigh crowed.

Samantha looked over to Lavinia and Brad. Brad seemed thoughtful. But Lavinia's pretty face was marred by an irritated frown. Samantha smiled as she patted Shining's foam-flecked neck.

"Guess we showed her," Samantha said to her filly.

She shook her head and smiled again. Maybe she and Shining would be ready to challenge Lavinia's filly after all!

THAT EVENING AFTER DINNER, SAMANTHA WAS SITTING AT the kitchen table surrounded by several cookbooks when Beth wandered in for a glass of water. Samantha sighed and said, "It's got to be perfect."

Beth sat down across from her and took a sip from her glass. "What exactly are you looking for?" she asked.

Samantha pushed her hair behind her ear and turned another page. "Something spectacular for my prom night dinner party. I can't even figure out what to serve for the main dish."

"Maybe I can help." Beth picked up one of the books and thumbed through it. "Well, you're probably not going to want anything too heavy, or you'll all be too weighted down to dance."

Samantha nodded. "I was thinking of something

47

light, like chicken, but all the recipes I've found are so spicy."

The two pored over the cookbooks for the next half hour but ended up rejecting every recipe they discussed. Finally, just as Samantha was ready to give up, she said, "I think I found one. Rosemary chicken stuffed with brown rice."

"Sounds good," Beth said, looking over Samantha's shoulder at the ingredients.

Samantha marked the book, but suddenly her face fell. "That's just the entrée!" she wailed. "Now I have to figure out what will go with it."

Beth leafed through another book. "Don't worry. Finding the entrée was the hard part. I'm sure these books will have some great vegetable dishes to go with it."

Samantha picked up another cookbook. "I can't believe there are only two days until the prom."

The afternoon of the prom, Samantha had just showered and slipped into a light cotton shirt and shorts when the doorbell rang.

Yvonne was grinning when Samantha opened the door and ushered her in. "We're going to have fun tonight," she said excitedly as she went into the kitchen and set down several bags of fresh fruit and vegetables.

"But we'd better get started," Samantha said with

a touch of nervousness. "We've got a lot to do. I've stuffed the chicken and laid out some of the table things. Come on. Let's go set the table."

She went into the dining room and opened the lower drawer in the china cabinet. She pulled out a white lace tablecloth. Yvonne's eyes grew wide.

"It's beautiful," Yvonne gasped, and reached out to touch the delicate cloth.

"It was my grandmother's," Samantha said, looking at it with misty eyes as she thought of her grandmother and her mother using the very same tablecloth.

She and Yvonne unfolded it and laid it out on the dining room table. Then Samantha carried over the crystal candlesticks and placed them in the center. The girls set six places with Samantha's mother's sterling silver. Next came the delicate place settings of fine bone china, also Samantha's mother's.

When everything was organized, the girls stood back to admire their handiwork. "Perfect," Yvonne declared.

But Samantha was looking thoughtfully at the center of the table. "Something's missing," she said. "I know. Flowers. I put a crystal vase out on the counter in the kitchen. Will you get that while I go cut some roses from the garden?"

A few minutes later Samantha came back into the cottage with an armload of sweet-smelling pink and white roses. She and Yvonne laughed and talked while they trimmed the stems and arranged the flowers in the vase. At last, the table was finished.

"Now it's perfect," Yvonne said.

The two girls spent the rest of the afternoon cutting vegetables and washing the raspberries that would be part of dessert.

"That about does it," Samantha said. "There's nothing left to do but get dressed, cook dinner, and wait for the guests to arrive."

Just then, the screen door banged open and Beth came into the kitchen. "I was coming over to see if I could help," she said as she glanced into the dining room. "But I see everything's already done. You two should be proud of yourselves. It looks wonderful." She sniffed the air appreciatively. "Smells yummy, too."

Yvonne and Samantha beamed proudly. The table did look good, Samantha thought. She glanced at the clock and winced. "Oh, no," she gasped. "Tor will be here in less than an hour. I'll never be ready."

Yvonne grabbed her car keys. "I'd better fly," she said. "I'll see you later."

"You run up and get dressed," Beth said. "I'll keep an eye on dinner."

Samantha waved good-bye to Yvonne and hurried to her room. She showered, then stepped into a light, silky slip and stockings. Next she put on the beautiful

50

jade-green dress that she'd bought in Lexington. She stood in front of the full-length mirror on her closet door and was pleased at her reflection. The flowing lines of the dress set off her figure and made the most of her five-foot, four-inch frame. And the color matched her green eyes perfectly.

Samantha headed for the bathroom and spent several minutes arranging her hair. When she was finished, she stood back and admired her handiwork. She'd managed to re-create the hairdo Ashleigh's sister, Caroline, had created for her for Ashleigh's wedding: her long red hair was swept down to one side so that curls cascaded down her cheek. Then she stepped into the low heels that matched her dress. As a final touch she put in her mother's tiny pearl earrings and placed a strand of lustrous pearls around her neck. She nodded as she surveyed herself critically in the mirror.

This was it! Samantha took a deep breath and started down the steps. Her father and Beth were in the living room, sitting on the sofa and waiting for her grand entrance. When she stepped into the room, they both rose and Beth cried, "You look absolutely beautiful!"

Her father's face was wreathed in smiles. "Beth's right, sweetheart. You look great." His eyes grew misty, and he stood up to give her a hug.

Cindy came into the room and stared when she

saw Samantha. "You look pretty," she said in awe.

"Thank you," Samantha said just as the doorbell rang. Tor was here! She took a deep breath and went to let him in. Tor stood on the doorstep, taking in Samantha with an admiring glance.

"Wow, Sammy," he said, stepping inside. "You look great."

"Thanks," Samantha said, suddenly feeling shy. Tor looked wonderful. He was wearing a snow-white tuxedo with a black bow tie. The white tux really set off his light tan. His blond hair was brushed back casually, and Samantha found herself wanting to push a stray lock off his forehead.

"You look pretty good yourself," Samantha said, turning her head so he wouldn't see her excited flush.

Tor held up a clear box with a corsage of tiny white rosebuds. "Guess I picked the right color," he said.

Samantha opened the box and held the delicate rosebuds up against the fabric of her jade-green dress. "It's perfect."

Tor's face reddened a bit, but he looked pleased.

Beth helped Samantha pin the corsage onto her dress. A few minutes later Yvonne, Gregg, and Maureen and her date, Josh, arrived. Yvonne was wearing a beautiful Spanish dress. The tight black bodice contrasted with the brilliant red skirt that fell in gathered ruffles down one side. It dipped below one knee and swooped above the knee on the other side. She had pulled her thick black hair into a bun at the base of her neck and had adorned it with a red rose. A fringed shawl was draped over one shoulder dramatically.

"Oh, Yvonne, it's spectacular!" Samantha cried. "You couldn't have bought anything that looked better."

Maureen grinned. "Gregg told her that at least two hundred times on the way over here."

Gregg looked at Yvonne tenderly. "It's true," he said.

"You all look great yourselves," Yvonne said firmly.

"The food!" Samantha suddenly exclaimed, rushing toward the kitchen. Everyone followed. "Yvonne, can you light the candles—and start the tape deck?"

Soon lively, soft strains of music filled the air. Tor and Gregg helped Samantha take food from the oven. They placed it in serving dishes and set it on the table. Maureen filled the crystal glasses on the table with nonalcoholic sparkling cider. Finally all that was left to do was sit down at the table and begin.

Samantha looked at the candlelit table. The crystal and silver sparkled in the soft light. She caught her breath. The whole room suddenly seemed so romantic. It was as if they were dining in the fanciest of restaurants, as if she'd instantly grown up and become an adult. She carefully covered the skirt of her dress with her napkin. Just then, Tor reached over and squeezed her hand. "I hope the rest of the night is as good as this," he said, turning his blue eyes to Samantha.

The dinner couldn't have gone better. Everyone exclaimed again and again over the beautiful table, and when the food was served, they complimented Samantha and Yvonne even more. Samantha, taking her first forkful, was almost surprised to discover how delicious it was. The chicken was tender, the vegetables cooked to just the right crispness. Dessert, a rich raspberry tart, topped off a perfect meal. When dinner was over, Mr. McLean and Beth insisted on cleaning up, and the laughing group of prom-goers headed out to the country club. Yvonne and Gregg went with Tor and Samantha in Tor's dad's sedan, following Maureen and Josh. They met up again in the parking lot and made their way into the room the senior class had reserved at the gracious old country club.

"What a gorgeous room!" Maureen exclaimed.

Samantha agreed. She looked around and took in the elegant high ceilings, the velvet-curtained windows, the sweeping seating area, and then the steps that led down to the huge wooden dance floor. There were gorgeously dressed couples everywhere, clustered in little groups at the tables and walking around the seating area, greeting their friends.

"There's our table," Tor said, acknowledging a wave from one of their friends seated near the center of the room.

Samantha and Tor made their way to the table, with Yvonne and Gregg following.

"We'll catch up with you in a while," Maureen said. "I want to introduce Josh to someone on the newspaper staff."

Samantha sat at the linen-covered table, Tor on one side and Yvonne on the other. She leaned toward Yvonne. "Can you believe this is us, dressed like this, sitting here at our senior prom?" she whispered to her best friend.

Yvonne's eyes sparkled. "It is pretty unbelievable."

The band started playing, and Tor took Samantha onto the dance floor. They moved around the room to the band's energetic beat and then started slow dancing as the band played a soft, romantic song. Samantha rested her cheek on Tor's shoulder and danced as if in a dream. She closed her eyes and breathed in Tor's tangy aftershave. She'd remember this night for the rest of her life.

After a while the music switched back to a faster song, and the action picked up on the dance floor. Song after song was played. Laughing and moving wildly to the beat with Tor, Samantha finally declared that she couldn't dance another step.

Tor smiled and nodded. "I was just about to say the same thing," he said. "These shoes are killing me."

He led her back to the table, where a few other people were sitting out some of the faster dances. A couple of the girls had slipped out of their shoes. Samantha looked down at her own aching feet and impulsively kicked off hers. The music was so insistent, however, that she and Tor got up again after only minutes and were back out on the dance floor.

After the prom king and queen were announced, Samantha noticed the guitarist from the band talking to Yvonne. Yvonne was smiling and nodding. After a minute the guitarist went back to the stage.

"I wonder what that was about," Samantha murmured to Tor.

Tor looked over at Yvonne. "I have a feeling we're about to find out."

He was right. Suddenly the room quieted, and the guitarist picked up an acoustic guitar. He did a couple of chords as the puzzled prom-goers watched. Soon they started whistling for the music to begin again. Yvonne waited.

Then the guitarist started up a flamenco beat. Yvonne started whirling and swirling and dipping, her feet moving in perfect time to the hypnotic, romantic music. Couples watched for a few seconds, almost bewitched by Yvonne's dark beauty and swirling black-and-red Spanish dress. One or two of the braver couples started imitating Yvonne's steps.

"Looks like fun," Tor said, reaching for Samantha. They exchanged smiles, then stepped out on the floor.

Nobody could move as fluidly as Yvonne, but it didn't matter. Amid missteps and near collisions, the laughing couples danced—or tried to—to the steps of the beautiful, haunting flamenco. When the dance was over, the crowd whistled and cheered.

"Way to go, Yvonne!" someone yelled across the floor.

Yvonne flushed, but then grabbed the red rose out of her hair and tossed it dramatically to Gregg.

Finally the prom-goers danced the last dance. The couples applauded wildly, and the senior class president said a few words, thanking the band and everyone who'd helped make the prom such a success. Samantha took one last look around the enchanted room and sighed. Tor's hand closed warmly over hers as they walked to the car. Yvonne and Gregg had decided to go home with Maureen and Josh, so Tor and Samantha were alone. In the soft moonlight, Tor pushed her curls back from her face and gave her a gentle kiss.

"Thank you for a wonderful night," he said.

Samantha smiled, happiness flooding through her. "Thank you," she whispered back.

They drove home, enjoying a companionable silence,

each lost in thought. At the doorstep Tor embraced Samantha warmly and their lips met in another tender kiss. Samantha could feel her heart flip-flopping.

"Have I told you before that I love you, Sammy?" Tor whispered.

"I love you too," she whispered back.

They kissed again. Finally Tor said a reluctant good night. Once he was gone, Samantha leaned against the doorframe and looked up at the starry night sky. She knew she'd never be able to fall asleep after such an exciting night. Even though she'd danced for hours, she was still full of energy. She went around to the back door, kicked off her dancing shoes, and stepped into her stable boots. She'd go down to see Shining and tell her all about her wonderful night.

5

AS SAMANTHA NEARED SHINING'S STALL SHE HEARD SOFT sobs coming from nearby. She walked over as quietly as she could, then spotted Cindy curled up beside the orphan foals, her hands covering her face, her small shoulders shaking.

She crouched down beside the girl and put her arm around her. "Cindy, what's wrong?"

Cindy looked up at Samantha, but the sobs didn't stop. "Shhh, shhh," Samantha comforted. "Things will be okay, Cindy. Tell me what happened."

"N-nothing h-happened," Cindy replied. "It's just that I like it here so much. Everyone is so nice to me, and I love all the horses. Tonight when I saw you all dressed up, and saw Beth and your dad smiling at you, it just seemed like there wasn't room for me here. I know they're going to make me leave, I just know it."

"Oh, Cindy, that's not true. We love having you here. My dad is doing everything he can to figure out how you can stay." Just then she noticed the same rumpled backpack Cindy had been using as a pillow the night Samantha first discovered her in the barn. *She must have been planning to run away again before she was sent away. How miserable she must feel*, Samantha thought. Samantha's eyes searched Cindy's face as she struggled to find the right words to comfort her.

"You can't leave Whitebrook yet, Cindy. There's so much you still haven't seen. Mr. Wonderful and Precocious are just about ready to start their training. And soon it will be time for the orphans to be halter-broken, and you'll want to help with that. And the Belmont Stakes race is coming up. We won't be going this year, but one of the colts Mike bred is running in it. We'll watch him run on TV, and everyone will be cheering, and . . ." She paused to see if Cindy was getting the picture. "And if you run away, you won't get to see the Pony Commandos. You'll miss seeing Mandy jump. Know what else? You wouldn't get to go with us to Churchill Downs to see Shining's next race."

Cindy's eyes filled again, and hastily she brushed at them with a dirty hand. "You—you mean you'd take me to see Shining race?" she asked in amazement.

Samantha nodded. "Of course. See what I mean?

There's so much you'd miss if you went away."

"But the Hadleys," Cindy said. "I'll get used to things and they'll just take me away, so what's the point?"

"You can't worry about how long they'll let you stay at Whitebrook," Samantha said. "Just enjoy each day here and see all you can. And don't give up that easily. Everyone here is fighting for you. We want you to stay."

"You really *do* want me to stay, don't you?" Cindy said wonderingly.

Samantha nodded solemnly. "We all do. Besides, I don't think Shining would forgive you if you left, or the orphans. They've grown so fond of you." Samantha smiled, surprised to find her own eyes misting. "Come on. It's late. Let's go to bed."

Saturday afternoon Samantha watched through the stall bars as Len showed Cindy how to halter-break the orphans.

"We take it very slowly," the old stable manager said. "We don't want to frighten these babies. If they get off to the wrong start, it'll take a lot of work to undo."

Len walked up to the first foal, who nuzzled the old man and butted against him. Len talked in a low voice and gently slipped the halter on in a deft movement, then buckled it. The foal looked with comical surprise at Len, then shook his head once or twice. He walked over to his brother on spindly legs and pressed up against him to try to rub the halter off. The other foal didn't cooperate. Instead he walked curiously up to Len, who handed the other halter to Cindy. "Go ahead," Len said. "Slowly. No sudden movements."

Cindy tried to imitate Len's easy manner, and she worked her way up to the second foal's head. She missed the first time she tried to slip on the halter, but on the second try she was successful.

"I did it," she said proudly.

"We'll have to name these guys soon," Len said.

"Come on, Cindy," Samantha called. "Let's go look in on Wonder. I promised Ashleigh I would. She's away for the afternoon at Townsend Acres. I hope Lavinia and Brad aren't around to give her a hard time."

"Who are they?" Cindy said.

"Brad is the son of the owner of Townsend Acres. That's where one of the horses Ashleigh half-owns is in training. Lavinia is Brad's wife. She makes trouble for us whenever she can because she hates it when our horses do better than hers."

Cindy took off and was trotting ahead down the barn aisle toward Wonder's stall.

Over the next few days Cindy's demeanor improved remarkably. Samantha was glad she'd had the opportunity to talk to her. It had obviously made a big difference.

"Cindy spends practically every minute down at the barn with Len and Vic, helping groom horses, washing and rolling bandages, cleaning tack, and holding the horses for the farrier," Samantha told Tor, Yvonne, and Gregg one evening when they all went out for cappuccino and dessert. "I've been helping her learn more about the horses, and she really is coming around. It's not like she's turned into Miss Sweetness and Light, but she's really a great, helpful kid."

"Sounds like she's had a pretty tough life," Yvonne said.

"Yeah, but now the horses are giving her something to hold on to," Tor observed.

Samantha sipped her cappuccino slowly. "She really took it seriously when I told her that the horses would miss her. She's been helping halter-break the orphans, and she spends a lot of time with Shining and me. She's finally started to open up a little."

"Do you think the child protection agency will let her stay?" Yvonne asked.

Samantha frowned. "I really don't know. But Beth's partner knows people who may be able to help. Beth is looking into what it takes to become a foster parent. She told me the state requires foster parents to take a training course. I just hope it all works out."

*   *   *

On Sunday morning Samantha got up early to work Shining. She had to make every moment around the horses count these days, because once finals started she wouldn't have much time for workouts.

Shining's breath misted in the cool morning air, and she pawed the ground anxiously as Samantha tacked her up.

"You're eager this morning, aren't you?" Samantha said, patting her filly's elegant neck. She rode her over to the grassy area by the training oval and waited for her turn to take the newly harrowed track.

Samantha listened to Ashleigh's last-minute advice before she pushed down her goggles and moved onto the track at a slow trot. Shining tossed her head, and Samantha closed her fingers on the reins as she proceeded with her warm-up. As she came off the far turn she watched for Ashleigh's sign. At a sharp nod of Ashleigh's head, Samantha rose in her stirrups and crouched over Shining's withers as the filly shot forward, her strides lengthening. Dirt clods flew up from the track as Samantha eased out the reins for a collected gallop. She held Shining at that pace for a while, and when they hit the half-mile pole, she crouched even lower, kneading her hands gently along Shining's neck. She was at a flat-out gallop now, and Samantha could hear the wind roaring in her ears as they continued down the stretch. They shot past Ashleigh, and Samantha closed her hands on the reins, gradually slowing Shining down to a canter. Finally she pulled up and made her way back to Ashleigh.

"You were really flying," Ashleigh said, grinning broadly. "Shining looked great. How'd she feel?"

"Like she could have gone on for another mile with ease!" Samantha beamed and patted her filly's neck. She'd already known that Shining's work had been stellar, but it felt good hearing it from Ashleigh. She gave a deep sigh of satisfaction as she headed off the track. After throwing her leg over the saddle and jumping to the ground, she walked Shining to cool her out. Cindy appeared out of nowhere, grooming box in hand.

"I'll groom her if you want," Cindy said.

"Thanks. That would be great."

Cindy took Shining's bridle and stood while Samantha slipped her halter and lead shank on.

"I've been reading the book you loaned me about Man o' War. It's really great. I never liked reading before."

Samantha smiled. "I'm glad you're enjoying it. You can borrow my books anytime."

Cindy grinned shyly. "Thanks. I'm going to read *The Manual of Horsemanship* next."

As Samantha turned to get another horse ready,

she thought about the reading she had to do for finals and sighed. Reading about horses was much more interesting.

The next afternoon after school Yvonne came over, and she and Samantha studied late into the evening, taking time out only to help with the evening feeding and to eat a quick dinner.

"I can't wait until finals are over." Yvonne groaned.

"You and me both," Samantha said. "Let's quiz each other again on that last chapter."

"Another one down!" she shouted to Yvonne the next afternoon as they walked out of class after their English final.

Yvonne moaned. "Yeah, but I just hope I did all right. Those essay questions gave me a headache."

They hurried through the crowded hallways, and Samantha was suddenly struck by the fact that her high school days were numbered. No more jostling her way through the halls of Henry Clay High School. She swallowed a lump in her throat and ducked into the door of the newspaper room to talk to Maureen about her final piece for the school paper.

"I thought you could write about Shining—your plans for her training, her future," Maureen said. "I figured that now that you have your very own racehorse, you'd want to write about her."

"There's nothing I'd rather write about. Maybe I can even include some information about jobs in the horse industry for the graduating class." Kentucky ranked first nationally in the breeding of Thoroughbreds, and many of Samantha's fellow students would probably end up working with horses.

The next morning Samantha rushed down to the barn and slipped a halter and lead shank on Shining. It was cool, a perfect morning for some light exercise. In only two weeks the filly would be racing again. Samantha thought she'd just do a couple of slow gallops around the track. It might be hard to hold Shining back, but once she got into the ease of the rhythm, she'd probably enjoy it. Samantha waved hello to Cindy, who was sitting on a hay bale, cleaning a double bridle. Cindy waved back, but she didn't stop her task to talk. Samantha had just saddled up and mounted and was walking toward the training oval when she heard Cindy say, "Hey, Samantha, stop a minute."

Puzzled, Samantha pulled up and turned toward Cindy. Cindy walked over, her brow furrowed as she looked intently at Shining's front legs. "It's this one," she said, pointing to Shining's right foreleg.

"This one what? What do you mean?" Samantha asked, her eyes following Cindy's gaze to the leg.

"She's walking funny. Not the way she usually does."

"Are you sure?" Samantha asked.

She urged Shining forward for a couple of steps, and then she could feel it. Shining was hesitating ever so slightly. Quickly Samantha dismounted. Cindy took Shining's bridle and held her while Samantha ran her hand up and down Shining's leg. She couldn't feel any heat or swelling. She made her way down to the hoof. Shining's hooves hadn't been in good shape when she'd arrived at Whitebrook, and maybe some long-forgotten condition was showing up. Samantha's mouth was dry as she examined the hoof. "I don't see anything," she said.

"Maybe she's got something under her shoe," Cindy suggested.

"Well, I'd better check it out," Samantha said thoughtfully. "I'll be right back."

She darted away for a minute, then returned carrying some farrier's tools. Carefully she removed the light racing shoe from Shining's right forefoot. She set it down, then examined the area underneath. "Look at this. You were right," she said, holding out a small pebble that had lodged under the shoe. It wasn't even as big as a pea, but it had obviously caused Shining discomfort, and the filly could have ended up lame if Samantha had galloped her.

"Good thinking, Cindy!" Samantha praised the girl. "Thanks for your help."

A small smile flickered on Cindy's lips, and once

again Samantha marveled over how much the girl had changed since she first arrived at Whitebrook.

Samantha untacked Shining and returned her to her stall. She'd have to have the shoe replaced before Shining could be worked again. As Samantha left the barn she saw Ashleigh in the stable yard.

"What's up?" Samantha asked.

"I've got some news for you," Ashleigh said. "Hank told me this morning that Lavinia's entered Her Majesty in the Lafayette at Churchill Downs, the same race Shining will be in. I don't think Lavinia knows Shining's running."

"Oh, no. We'll be running against Her Majesty?" Samantha exclaimed. She felt her heart thud in her chest. Sure, she had a lot of faith in Shining, but Her Majesty was more experienced. Could Shining hold her own against Lavinia's expensive horse?

Her doubt must have registered in her face, because Ashleigh squared her shoulders determinedly. "Shining won't disgrace herself. She doesn't have Wonder's blood running through her for nothing!"

Samantha smiled gratefully at her friend. She and Shining would simply have to put everything they had into getting ready for the race. "Well, maybe Shining won't be able to beat Her Majesty," she said. "But she's in top shape and she'll put her heart into it. She'll put in a performance to be proud of."

Ashleigh nodded. "That's the way to think."

Samantha looked off into the rolling hills, already beginning to plan how she'd get the most out of the training time left between now and the race. She glanced over to Ashleigh. "Will you have time to ride her in a couple of workouts this week?" she asked.

"You bet I will," Ashleigh said. "I want to beat Lavinia as much as you do."

Just then they saw Cindy walk from the mares' barn over to the paddock where the orphan foals were turned out. She was holding Flurry.

Ashleigh turned to Samantha. "Any news on Cindy's future?"

Samantha shook her head. "Nope, we still haven't heard anything. I'm still trying to get her to open up a little bit, tell me about her past. It's not easy, but I know we could get through to her if we just had some time."

Ashleigh nodded. "Well, now looks like a good time to try to talk to her. I'll see you later."

Samantha walked over to Cindy and set down her bucket. "Hi. What's going on?"

"Nothing," Cindy said, gently stroking the cat. "Just thinking."

"About what?"

Cindy kept her eyes on the cat. Samantha could see a single tear make its way down her cheek.

"I was thinking about my parents."

"You must miss them," Samantha said gently.

Cindy nodded. "Do you think it will ever stop hurting?"

Samantha looked searchingly at her. "I lost my mom when I was twelve. She was killed in a riding accident. The sadness never completely goes away, but I go on. Life goes on, and I try to work at becoming what I know she'd want me to be."

Cindy wiped at her tear. "I never really thought of it that way."

"It's not always easy," Samantha admitted. "But there are people who care about you and understand how you feel." Cindy nodded and went back to stroking the cat. Samantha went back to her chores, leaving the girl alone with her thoughts.

OVER THE NEXT FEW DAYS IT SEEMED TO SAMANTHA THAT she had never been busier. Every morning she was up before dawn, working Shining on the training oval or watching Ashleigh take the filly around for her workouts. Then she was at school, taking another final, and after school, when the stable chores were finished, she was up late working on her school newspaper column.

"Hooray! One more day, then graduation," she said to Yvonne one afternoon after they'd both taken their last final.

"Yeah, it's good-bye, Henry Clay High, hello, University of Kentucky," Yvonne said. "I'll kind of miss the place."

As the girls headed toward their lockers Mr. Lochrie, Henry Clay's head counselor, stepped into the hallway and waved at Samantha to come into the office.

Samantha took a deep breath and opened the glass door.

Mr. Lochrie's face broke into a wide grin as she entered the office.

"Well, Samantha, you happened by at just the right time," he said. "You're graduating in the top ten percent of your class."

Samantha blinked. "Re-really?" she stammered. Her grades had been pretty good throughout her years at Henry Clay, but she'd never dreamed she'd be among the top students. What great news. Her dad would be thrilled, but not half as thrilled as she was! She ran out of the office to tell Yvonne.

Yvonne whooped and hugged her friend, and congratulated Samantha over and over again. They'd just finished cleaning out their lockers when Maureen came running down the hall, her cheeks flushed and her eyes sparkling. "I made it too," she called out breathlessly. "Mr. Lochrie just told me."

She looked over at Yvonne, afraid that maybe she'd hurt Yvonne's feelings. It was no secret that Yvonne wasn't the world's best student.

"Don't worry about me," Yvonne said cheerfully. "I never studied half as hard as I should have. But I'm proud of you guys. You deserve to celebrate."

The girls looked at each other. "Frozen yogurt!" Maureen yelled.

The three friends piled into Maureen's car and drove over to Yogurt Blues, where they sat down to enormous dishes of Wailin' Praline frozen yogurt.

The next afternoon Samantha and Cindy drove over to Tor's stable for the Pony Commandos' lesson. She and Tor and Beth, Janet, Gregg, and Yvonne assisted the six young riders onto their ponies. Samantha watched the students quietly as they went around the large indoor ring. After a while she noticed that an extremely pretty blond girl was standing by the gate. Her eyes seemed to be riveted on Tor.

"Who's that?" Samantha asked Yvonne. "I haven't seen her before."

"That's Angelique Dubret," Yvonne answered. "The new boarder with that super warmblood. She's been getting a lot of extra coaching from Tor—not that she needs it. She's an incredible rider."

Samantha started thoughtfully at the girl a moment longer, then turned her attention back to the Pony Commandos.

"Did we do well?" Mandy asked, pulling up Butterball in front of Samantha after they'd cantered.

Samantha reached out and patted Butterball's muzzle, then smiled at the little girl.

"You get better and better every time you ride," she said.

Mandy beamed before riding off. Samantha's gaze drifted over to where Cindy was leaning up against the rail, watching the children. If only she were able to get through to Cindy the way she was able to get through to Mandy. Samantha knew from their last discussion that there was a great deal of emotion simmering under Cindy's rough exterior. Well, Samantha decided, she could be patient if she had to be. She had time.

Glancing up, she saw a car she didn't recognize pull into the drive behind the stable. Her father's car was right behind. Samantha's gaze slid automatically to Cindy. This had to be about her. What else would bring Mr. McLean to Tor's stable?

"Tor, can you take over for a few minutes?" she asked. "I'll be right back."

She walked over to Cindy.

"That's Mrs. Lovell," Cindy said quietly as a tall, thin woman in a navy suit climbed out of the first car.

Samantha saw her dad get out of his car and talk to the woman.

"They must be here to get me," Cindy said, the color draining from her cheeks.

"We don't know that," Samantha said, trying not to let Cindy see how nervous she was.

She placed her arm around Cindy's shoulders as they walked toward her father and Mrs. Lovell and was pleased when Cindy didn't shake it off.

"This is Mrs. Lovell from Child Protection Services," Mr. McLean explained quietly to Samantha so no one else would hear. "She walked around Whitebrook and wanted to come here to talk with Cindy. She told me that the Hadleys still want Cindy to come back." He looked at Cindy, answering her unspoken question. "No one is going anywhere today."

Samantha refrained from letting her breath out in a whoosh of relief. She watched as Mrs. Lovell's dark eyes darted around, taking in everything around her.

"I'd better get back to the Commandos," Samantha said awkwardly, not sure of what to do next.

Her dad looked at her and nodded. "That's fine," he said. "Cindy will join you shortly."

Samantha gave Cindy one last reassuring glance, then walked back to the ring, where the Commandos were now trotting over poles placed on the ground.

"What's going on?" Tor asked Samantha after the class was over.

"I guess the Hadleys are still pushing to get Cindy back, and Mrs. Lovell, the caseworker from Child Protection Services, came to check things out," Samantha explained.

Tor nodded. "Well, it makes sense. She probably wants to see where Cindy spends her time when she's not at Whitebrook, and meet everyone and make sure Cindy's really happy."

Samantha sighed with relief as Mrs. Lovell got into the car and drove off.

"Is everything okay?" she asked as Cindy and her dad approached her.

Mr. McLean ruffled Cindy's hair. "Cindy kept telling Mrs. Lovell that she wanted to stay at Whitebrook, and Mrs. Lovell kept explaining to her that it might not be possible. I'm going to call Mrs. Lovell later and see if we can't put an end to this nonsense once and for all."

"I have to go see Mandy and help her with Butterball," Cindy said, breaking away and heading toward the little girl.

Mr. McLean watched her go. "Mrs. Lovell isn't totally convinced I'd make a good foster parent. She keeps reminding me that I'm single," he said when Cindy was out of earshot. "And she wasn't sure that it's safe for a child to be around high-strung racehorses all day long. But I think watching you and your friends work with the kids might have changed her mind about that."

"Will they let her stay?" Samantha asked anxiously.

Her father nodded. "For now. But I have to go down to their offices next week and sign yet more papers, if you can believe it. What a load of red tape," he grumbled before climbing back into his car. "See you back at Whitebrook."

"Your dad's got a lot on his mind," Tor observed.

Samantha nodded. "Yeah. But he's become fond of

Cindy. He knows what it's like to lose someone, and his heart goes out to people in trouble." As she spoke she looked over Tor's shoulder and saw Angelique ride into the ring on her beautiful blood-bay warmblood. The horse had to be close to seventeen hands, but he had beautiful conformation.

Tor turned and saw Angelique, too. He lifted a hand in greeting. "I'll be with you in a sec," he said to her.

Angelique smiled. "Okay. I'll warm him up."

Before Samantha had a chance to ask Tor about the special sessions he was giving Angelique, Mandy called excitedly from the edge of the ring.

"Sammy! Come and see what Cindy and I did to Butterball's mane! He looks so pretty."

Samantha couldn't refuse the warmhearted little girl's request. She'd have to wait to find out more about Angelique. "Coming," she called. "See you later," she added to Tor, who smiled, then turned his attention to his new boarder, who was riding her mount through perfect warm-up figures.

On graduation day the Kentucky sunshine shone brilliantly on the football field, where a platform had been set up to seat the graduating seniors. There were colorful flowers everywhere. Samantha and her friends stood talking in nervous clumps, admiring their graduation robes and waiting to line up and march to the platform. Once the music started, Samantha took a deep breath of the perfumed air and marched solemnly to her seat. Her eyes grew misty as she looked at her friends in their mortarboards. They looked so serious and so mature.

As the strains of "Pomp and Circumstance" swelled, Samantha looked around and saw her father and Beth sitting on the folding chairs that had been placed on the field. They were beaming with pride. Samantha's gaze moved on to where Tor was sitting. He gave her a wink and grinned at her. Samantha felt herself tingle. She was so glad he was here to see her proud moment. Straining a little, she could see Cindy sitting between Tor and Beth, dressed in a pretty flowered dress that Beth had bought for her in Lexington a few days before. Samantha turned back to listen to the valedictorian give her speech.

When the last diploma had been handed out, deafening cheers filled the air as the seniors threw their mortarboards up to the sky.

"We're so proud of you," Beth said, running up to Samantha afterward.

Mr. McLean stood with his hands in his pockets. He didn't need to say anything. Samantha could tell by his face how proud he was.

"I brought you something," Cindy said in a small voice.

Surprised, Samantha looked at the girl. She held

up a small horseshoe that had been painted with shiny silver paint. It had a silk cord tied onto it through the nail holes.

"It's for good luck," Cindy said. "Len helped me make it. It's really from Shining."

Samantha took the shoe and turned it over and over in her hand. She leaned forward and gave Cindy a hug.

"Thank you," she said. "This means a lot to me."

Cindy smiled and ducked her head. Tor stepped in with his congratulations.

Maureen had planned a post-graduation party, and after the last congratulations were made, they all hurried to her house. A local band played the latest songs, and the seniors danced and partied late into the night.

When Samantha got up the next morning at dawn, she knew it was time to focus all her energy on Shining's upcoming race. Lavinia had popped over to Whitebrook a couple of times recently to check on Shining's progress. When she found out about Cindy, she had asked Ashleigh how Mike felt about having a "juvenile delinquent" around the place. She also managed to get in plenty of digs about how well Her Majesty was doing, and how Shining didn't stand a chance against her.

"Don't worry," Ashleigh said after a great workout

with Shining. "Her Majesty will be eating Shining's dust."

"I hope so," Samantha said nervously as she carefully groomed and massaged the filly.

That afternoon Yvonne came over, and the two girls took Shining out on a walk around the pasture trails to give her a change of scenery.

"We need to relax her before her big day," Samantha explained. "Only four days to go."

Cindy was waiting for them at the barn when they got back. She had a bucket of warm water, and she sponged Shining down, then groomed her and cleaned out her hooves. Samantha tried to start a conversation, but Cindy just shrugged and turned back to Shining. She still had a long way to go before she would allow anyone to get close to her. In fact, Samantha thought, Cindy had clammed up again since Mrs. Lovell's visit to the stable.

The next day when Samantha returned with Shining after a walk, Cindy stood as usual, bucket in hand.

"Here you are," Samantha said, handing Shining's lead rope to the girl. On her way out of the barn she passed Wonder's stall and noticed that her light summer sheet was hanging slightly askew. Ducking inside, she started to adjust the blanket. From there she could hear Cindy talking in a low voice to Shining as she groomed her in the crossties.

"I know people don't think horses are smart," Cindy half-whispered to the horse. "But you're smart—you're smarter than most people I know. I like horses better than people, too. You know the worst thing about all the foster homes I've lived in? It was knowing that I'd never stay in any one of them for very long. There was never any point in getting to know anyone, because after a while I'd just have to leave. You understand, don't you, girl? Samantha told me about you. They treated you badly at that other stable, didn't they? Well, if we're lucky, maybe I'll get to stay here and we can be together for a long, long time. I hope so. I really like it here."

When Cindy finally finished grooming Shining and led her back to her stall, Samantha stood quietly behind Wonder, thinking about the sad life the young girl had known.

"We won't let them take her away, will we, girl?" she whispered to Wonder, who nodded her lovely head up and down several times as if in agreement.

Later that evening, after Cindy had drifted off to sleep on the couch, Samantha went into the kitchen and described some of what she'd heard to Beth, who listened with concern.

"I had an idea, which I talked over with your dad," Beth said. "Cindy's been sleeping on the couch for several weeks. She's never complained, but it can't be comfortable. I thought we could clear out that back room. Janet said she had an extra twin bed we could have. We can set up the room as a bedroom for Cindy. It'll give her the feeling that we all really mean for her to stay."

"That's a great idea!" Samantha exclaimed. "Let's get to work."

"WE'RE OFF!" SAMANTHA SANG OUT AS THE BIG WHITE-
brook van pulled away from the stable yard and
made its way onto the road leading to Louisville.

Her dad grinned at her. "Well, just sit back and
relax, because we're going to take it slow," he said.
"The lady wants a smooth ride."

"Shining's ready, Dad," Samantha said. "Did you
see how eagerly she loaded this morning?"

Mr. McLean nodded. "She knows she's going to
race."

Samantha leaned back, closed her eyes, and pictured the track at Churchill Downs. It was an hour-
and-a-half drive to the famous racetrack, and the time
sped by as Samantha daydreamed about Shining's
glory. The filly had really thrown her heart into her
final workouts. Samantha smiled, thinking of how

Her Majesty would have her work cut out for her when she ran against Shining.

When they arrived, her father swung the van into Churchill Downs's backside, with its rows and rows of stables. Samantha's stomach lurched when she saw the Townsend Acres van rumble past them. That meant that Her Majesty was already here.

I hope I can avoid Lavinia, she thought grimly as she leaped out of the cab and walked to the back of the van. Fortunately the Whitebrook reserved stabling was nowhere near Townsend Acres's stabling. Samantha didn't have time to worry about Lavinia or her horse for the next several hours while she got Shining settled in her roomy box stall, and she didn't see anyone from Townsend Acres.

When Samantha arrived at the track before dawn the next morning, a light gray mist had settled over the backside. Samantha shivered in her light windbreaker as she walked to Shining's stall. Ashleigh was already there, talking to Mike as they checked a horse Mike had vanned over the night before. "Hi, Sammy," Ashleigh called cheerfully as Samantha unlatched Shining's stall door.

"It's pretty foggy," Samantha said glumly. "I wonder what the visibility will be on the track."

"The fog should lift. It almost always does in June. Anyway, the race is tomorrow, not today." She looked more closely at Samantha. "You seem down," she said. "Anything wrong?"

"Just nerves, I guess," Samantha admitted. "After all, this is only Shining's second race. Anything could happen."

Ashleigh swung into Shining's saddle. "Nothing to be nervous about," she said firmly. "We're going to go out there right now and show Shining this track. And tomorrow she'll own it."

Samantha smiled, grateful for Ashleigh's confidence in her beloved horse. She walked over to the rail to watch Shining's workout. The fluttering in her stomach calmed as she saw how quickly Shining seemed to take to the track surface. Samantha didn't even need a stopwatch to know that the fractions Shining set were more than respectable.

When Ashleigh pulled up and walked Shining over to where Samantha stood, she smiled. "See? What did I tell you? Shining's ready."

Samantha smiled. "Decent," she admitted. But a moment later she saw Her Majesty being ridden toward the track by a tall, thin exercise rider she didn't recognize. She eagerly went to the rail to watch Her Majesty's work while Len led Shining off to cool her out. Her Majesty worked well, and Samantha felt a stab of nervous apprehension as she and Ashleigh walked back to the barn area. Shining was going to have to run very well if she was going to beat Her Majesty.

The next morning Samantha found that her stomach was fluttering even more. She tried to talk to herself to calm her nerves as she gave Shining a meticulous grooming in the pale morning sun.

"You are going to be brilliant," she said to her horse. "The track is perfect, your workouts have been great, and everyone is coming to see you."

"That's right," said a familiar voice.

Samantha spun around. It was Tor, walking toward her with Ashleigh. At the sight of her friends, Samantha relaxed a little. Tor gave her a light kiss.

Ashleigh's eyes swept critically over Shining. "She looks good," she said. "She's going to put in a good performance today, I just know it."

Tor agreed. "She likes it here," he added. "You can tell."

Samantha glanced at Shining, who seemed relaxed but alert. Her eyes took in every detail, her ears flicking back and forth at the sounds around her. It was clear that she felt quite comfortable at Churchill Downs.

"I think you're right," Samantha said, turning back to finish brushing Shining's gleaming coat.

"Mrs. Jarvis and Mandy will be here soon." Tor ran a hand over Shining's shoulder.

"Great," Samantha said. "And my dad and Beth are bringing Yvonne and Cindy."

"It'll be a real treat for Cindy," Ashleigh commented.

Samantha nodded, then collected her grooming tools and returned them to the tack box.

A few minutes later Ian McLean and Beth arrived with Cindy and Yvonne.

"Hi, Cindy," Samantha said, watching her take in the sights and sounds of the gracious old racetrack.

"Hi," Cindy said shyly. But her eyes were shining with excitement, and Samantha could tell she was thrilled to be included in the day's activities. Cindy walked over to Shining and let her whoof softly into her palm, then she rubbed the filly's forehead and whispered something into her ear.

Mrs. Jarvis and Mandy showed up an hour later. Mandy's hair was pulled back in a ponytail and tied with a blue ribbon to match her blue dress. She made her way over to Shining. "She looks so beautiful," she said, reaching up to stroke Shining's nose.

Samantha smiled, warmed even more by the sight of the girl. Everyone believed in Shining, she told herself. That had to be a good sign. Still, she wished that the butterflies in her stomach would go away once and for all.

Ashleigh turned to Samantha. "There's quite a bit of time left until the race," she said. "I know how queasy I get when one of my horses is running. And it always makes me feel better if I can just get a change of scenery for a while. I'll stay here with Shining. Why don't you walk around a little? Cindy would probably enjoy a tour of Churchill Downs, don't you think?"

Samantha glanced at Shining, then at Cindy, and nodded. "Lead the way," Yvonne said.

For a while Samantha was able to forget her worries as she watched Mandy and Cindy. Cindy had a comment to make about every horse, and her love of the animals seemed even more evident than usual.

"You know, Cindy," Samantha said, "I've been meaning to ask you if you'd like to learn to ride sometime."

"You really mean it?"

Samantha smiled at her enthusiasm. "I do . . . if you're interested."

"I am," Cindy said, giving her a genuine smile.

"Then we'll do it soon. I promise." Samantha cheered up momentarily, but her stomach started churning again the minute they returned to Shining's stall.

"It's getting close to race time," Len said.

Samantha nodded and hurried off to change into a light summer dress. Normally she didn't really care what she wore, but as Shining's owner and trainer, she wanted to look her best.

"Wow, Sammy, great dress," Tor said admiringly when she returned.

"Thanks," Samantha said distractedly.

Tor hugged her and gave her a thumbs-up. "Relax.

Shining will do herself proud," he said. "She's been trained well, she's feeling good, and she looks ready. Don't you worry."

Samantha gave him a grateful smile as she took Shining's lead shank. The filly looked gorgeous. Her roan coat was covered with a blue-and-white satin sheet emblazoned with the Whitebrook name. Although she was Shining's owner, Samantha had decided to race the filly under Whitebrook's colors. Ashleigh had already left for the jockeys' rooms.

Fifteen minutes before the race Samantha led Shining to the saddling paddock and walking ring. Len held the filly while Samantha saddled her. Suddenly a piercing voice cut through the air. Samantha cringed as she caught a glimpse of Lavinia, several stalls down.

"Did you see the odds?" Lavinia exclaimed loudly. "Her Majesty's the favorite."

The last odds Samantha had seen were in Her Majesty's favor. Shining, with only one win in April, was listed as 8 to 1. There were six other fillies in the race.

The jockeys entered the walking ring as Samantha took Shining out of the saddling box. Hank, the head groom at Townsend Acres and a good friend of Samantha's, was leading Her Majesty. He nodded when he saw her, giving her a broad grin and a wink.

Samantha returned the smile, then looked over at

Her Majesty. There was no denying the strapping dapple-gray filly was gorgeous. Shining was smaller in comparison, but Samantha lifted her chin. Size didn't necessarily mean anything. Heart and talent were all that counted on the track.

Giving Ashleigh a leg into the saddle, Samantha tried to smile bravely.

Ashleigh settled and adjusted her light racing cap. "Hey, don't look so frightened, Sammy," she said reassuringly. "Shining isn't going to embarrass herself, are you, girl? *Clunker's* not in her vocabulary today."

Shining nickered softly. Samantha gave her filly an affectionate kiss on the nose. "Just do your best," she whispered. "That's all that matters."

She watched as the jockeys and horses headed out to the track through the passage under the grandstand. She glanced at Her Majesty's jockey, Le Blanc. He was a skillful and shrewd jockey, Samantha knew. But so was Ashleigh.

A few minutes later Samantha was seated in Whitebrook's reserved seating, her binoculars trained on the field as the horses warmed up. She wished Her Majesty didn't look so good.

Tor put his arm around her reassuringly. "She'll do fine," he murmured, giving her a little squeeze.

Samantha closed her eyes. All her dreams for Shining were coming together, and she prayed everything would go right.

"They're loading," Mandy whispered excitedly.

Samantha tensed as she watched Shining being loaded into the number-five spot. The gates flipped open as the starting bell rang, and eight Thoroughbred fillies surged out onto the track. Samantha breathed a sigh of relief as Shining broke cleanly and sharply. A horse could get a bad break and never recover ground. But Shining was up close to the lead.

"This race is a mile," Samantha heard Tor explaining to Cindy. "Samantha's been gradually increasing the distance that Shining runs."

"It's Deco in the lead," came the announcer's voice over the loudspeaker system. "Gaining on her steadily is Shining, ridden by Ashleigh Griffen."

Samantha raised her binoculars again and watched as Ashleigh expertly angled the filly in closer to the rail. Her Majesty, who liked to run slightly off the pace, was back in fourth. As they went into the first turn Ashleigh held Shining back in second. The lead horse, Deco, increased her lead on the field slightly to a length and a half, but Samantha wasn't concerned. She knew Ashleigh was waiting for her moment. Another filly, Copper Wash, was gaining slightly on Shining's outside. Her Majesty was still in fourth behind Shining on the rail.

The horses pounded down the backstretch toward the far turn. Shining began eating into Deco's lead.

"Yes! Yes!" Samantha cried, but her eye was on

Her Majesty as well. Surprisingly, the filly didn't seem to be putting in a run. She was still on the rail, now two lengths behind Shining as other horses began moving up through the pack.

As they entered the far turn Ashleigh edged Shining outside of Deco, and they passed the other filly. Samantha was so excited, she could hardly breathe. "Go, Shining!" she cried. "Oh, come on, baby!"

Mandy started jumping up and down, and Cindy stood up and chewed her fingernail as she watched the other horses moving up, too. Copper Wash moved up to challenge for second. Two late closers began moving up outside of Her Majesty. Her Majesty finally changed gears and started gaining ground.

"Le Blanc's looking for an opening," Tor said.

"Come on, Shining!" yelled Mandy.

"You can do it!" Cindy shouted.

Samantha felt her tension increase as Her Majesty continued gaining. Her eyes never left the field as Deco finally started running out of steam and Copper Wash moved past the tiring horse. Le Blanc immediately urged Her Majesty around Deco. But a black filly, Bon Soir, was coming up fast on his outside. The two horses seemed to bump shoulders, but Samantha wasn't sure; it all had happened so fast.

Coming down the stretch, Shining had the lead by a length. Samantha jumped to her feet. "Just another sixteenth, girl!" she shouted encouragingly. "Come on now! You can do it."

"And at the sixteenth pole," the announcer cried, "it's Shining by a length, but Her Majesty has found *her* best stride and is moving up quickly on the outside to challenge Copper Wash. Those two are neck and neck. But Shining is digging in. The filly has *more!* As they approach the wire it's Shining by a length and a half, Her Majesty and Copper Wash still vying for second. They're not going to catch Shining today. And as they cross the finish line it's Shining by a length and three quarters! Then Her Majesty and Copper Wash in what looks like a dead heat for second. An impressive performance for this lightly raced filly to outrun one of the top three-year-old fillies in the country."

"Shining won!" Mandy shouted. She reached over and grabbed Cindy in an exuberant bear hug. Cindy forgot her usual reserve and hugged the little girl back.

Samantha hugged Tor and Mandy and Cindy. "I can't believe it! She's so amazing!"

"Shining did it, Shining did it!" Mandy and Cindy said over and over, jumping up and down.

Just then the inquiry sign flashed on the board. Shining's number was illuminated in the first spot. The photo sign was flashing for the place and show spots.

"I wonder what the inquiry's about," Tor said. "Did you notice anything, Sammy?"

"It looked like Her Majesty and that black filly may have bumped coming into the turn," Samantha said. "But I wasn't sure."

As Samantha and Tor hurried down to the winner's circle, Samantha could hear the commotion swirling around her.

"Le Blanc's registered a protest against Bon Soir's jock for bumping him on the turn," she heard someone in the crowd say. "He claims it caused Her Majesty to lose her momentum and lose the race."

"I don't know what Le Blanc hopes to gain by making a protest," Tor said in a low voice. "They finished way ahead of Bon Soir, and it looks like they've won the photo." He glanced over to the infield board, where Her Majesty's number was glowing in the place spot, Copper Wash's in show. "Even if Bon Soir's disqualified, it's not going to affect Her Majesty's finishing position."

"Probably Lavinia stirring up trouble," Samantha said. But she had more important things on her mind, like congratulating her filly and Ashleigh. She hugged Shining as Ashleigh rode her into the winner's circle. "I'm so proud of you, girl! What a fantastic race!"

She beamed as she stood for the photos. She'd never felt more proud. Samantha gave Shining another affectionate hug. "You did it, girl," she said softly. "You definitely showed them your stuff."

Samantha walked on clouds for the next week. Granted, Shining had only won a small stakes race, but they'd beaten Her Majesty! The stewards had decided against Le Blanc; they didn't feel Bon Soir's interference was enough to have cost Her Majesty the race.

"Of course, that doesn't make Lavinia happy," Ashleigh said when she caught up with Samantha at the trainers' office at the end of the week. "She's telling everyone that her filly would have won if she hadn't been bumped."

"She just can't admit that Shining ran a better race," Samantha said. She shrugged. "Well, this means just one thing. Here we go again. The pressure's really going to be on if Shining and Her Majesty race against each other again."

8

"SO, WHAT DO YOU SAY, CINDY?" SAMANTHA SAID A WEEK after Shining's triumph at Churchill Downs. "Are you ready to ride?"

Cindy looked down at the new black boots and tan breeches Beth had bought for her. She nodded and pushed a wisp of her blond hair off her face. She'd put her hair back in a ponytail with one of Samantha's ribbons, but a few thin strands had escaped.

"You sure gave those boots a nice polish," Samantha complimented the young girl. "And your breeches fit perfectly. You look like a model from a riding catalog."

At that, Cindy lifted her chin.

"You'll do fine," Samantha said reassuringly, handing her a helmet. "You know Shining. She may be a racehorse on a track, but in a regular riding ring she's a pussycat, a gentle riding horse. She'll take good care of you."

Samantha led the way to the tack room, feeling that the timing of the lesson couldn't have been more perfect. In the last few days her father had gone down to the Child Protection Services offices several times in an effort to convince Mrs. Lovell that though he was a single parent, he was doing a good job caring for Cindy. He'd taken Beth with him, and each time they'd returned, they looked tired and worried. "They seem to be stuck on this single-parent theme," Mr. McLean said. "I think it's time to hire a lawyer." He kept Cindy abreast of each development, telling her honestly in a gentle way, trying to still her fears without making promises. Cindy had retreated more and more to the stables, spending whole afternoons with the orphans. It had been Ashleigh who'd suggested to Samantha that Shining was rested enough from her race to take Cindy for her first riding lesson.

"She needs to get her mind off her problems," Ashleigh told Samantha.

After carefully studying the saddles that were placed in neat rows in the tack room, Samantha selected a saddle with a deep seat for Cindy. "This will give you a real feeling of security," she said. And she showed Cindy the special stirrups that had breakaway sides. "Tor and I use this kind of equipment with our young riders."

Cindy examined them, then took the grooming box and followed Samantha to Shining's stall. They groomed the filly and tacked her up. Cindy took Shining out to the ring where they longed and trained young horses, Samantha walking next to them.

"What if I do the wrong thing?" Cindy asked fearfully after she'd gotten a leg up into the saddle and Samantha was showing her how to adjust her stirrup leathers.

"Shining's very forgiving," Samantha said soothingly. "So don't you worry about it. Now put the ball of your foot in the iron, like that. Now take your reins like this." She showed Cindy how to hold the reins. "And sit back deep in your seat. There. That's it."

Cindy followed Samantha's instructions intently. "Sit so that your weight is centered over Shining's back. Let her know that you're in charge," Samantha continued. "Sit up tall. Pretend that there's a string pulling you up by the top of your hard hat, and it's pulling your back straight, straighter. You've got it.

"Chin up, square your shoulders. Now for a very important part," Samantha went on. "Let your weight sink into your stirrups so that your heels are down. Perfect. We're just going to walk today to get you used to the motion. Now gently squeeze with your heels to nudge Shining forward. Don't worry. I'll stay right at her head."

Samantha watched as Cindy bit her lip and, trying to maintain her form, squeezed with her heels. Shining flicked her ears back and moved forward obediently. She seemed to know how fearful Cindy was, and she moved out fluidly and slowly. Cindy began to relax as they made their way down the rail.

"Heels down," Samantha reminded her as she glanced at her stirrups. Cindy immediately jammed down her heels, startling Shining. She stopped short and tossed her head. Cindy's face turned white.

"I did something wrong," she said.

"Cindy, relax. It's your first time. Just remember to be gentle," Samantha said. "A well-trained horse like Shining responds to the slightest movement."

Cindy breathed in and brushed back a lock of sweaty hair that had escaped from under her cap. "There's a lot to remember all at once, isn't there?" she asked.

"Yes," Samantha said. "But once you get the hang of it, you won't have to think about all the details."

Samantha saw that Cindy's face brightened, and this time when she adjusted her foot in the stirrup, she did so in a barely perceptible movement.

After a couple of rounds Samantha told Cindy that she would go stand in the center of the paddock while Cindy made circuits around her. "You're doing well. Now let's see you take Shining around by yourself."

Cindy nodded and walked on, her thin shoulders squared, her back ramrod straight. She followed Samantha's instructions to the letter, trying to ride as perfectly as possible as she went around the paddock for a few more circuits. Samantha noted the determined set of her jaw and was reminded of another determined rider—Mandy Jarvis. "You're doing fine," she called to Cindy. "Now relax, and have some fun while you're at it. That's what riding's really all about.

"Should we call it a day?" Samantha asked when she noticed that Cindy was getting tired. "You've done really well for your first time."

Cindy smiled and nodded, reaching out to pet Shining as she let out her breath in a huge sigh of relief. "There's still so much to learn," she said. "And I want to learn it all."

Samantha laughed. Cindy's intensity was so much like her own at that age. She nodded. "You will," she said. "I know you will."

"There must be some books I could read that tell you how to ride," Cindy said as they started back to the barn.

"I have a couple of good ones I'll lend you," Samantha said. She reached out to stroke Shining's silky mane. The filly had behaved perfectly with Cindy, treating her as if she were made of glass. Samantha's heart swelled in gratitude.

"You know," she said casually, "if you like, you can help me get Shining in top condition for her next race."

Cindy turned in her saddle, interested. "Great. I loved watching her run. When's her next race?"

"In August," Samantha said. "We're going to go up to Saratoga for a couple of weeks. Mike and Ashleigh have some horses running. And Sierra will be racing there, too—he's entered in two steeplechases."

"Oh," Cindy said softly.

"And Mike's sprinter Blues King will be running in a big stakes race. It should be really exciting."

A cloud seemed to pass over Cindy's face. "You'll all be going away for two weeks?" she asked with a catch in her voice.

Samantha nodded and suddenly understood the unspoken question in Cindy's words. Where would she be in a few weeks? It must be awful to have to live with the uncertainty. Samantha wanted to bite her tongue. She wished she'd never mentioned Saratoga at all.

"Oh, it's a month or so off," she said lightly. "Hey, look. There's Len. We've got to tell him about your lesson. He'll be pleased to hear how well you rode."

After chatting with Len for a moment, Samantha helped Cindy bathe and groom Shining. Cindy was silent as she went about her work even though

Samantha tried to keep up a light conversation about riding. After Shining was settled back in her stall, Cindy said, "I'm going to work with the orphans," and disappeared.

Samantha sighed. It was clear that the glow of Cindy's first riding lesson had been dimmed by the news about Saratoga. Maybe they could find a way to take Cindy with them.

Samantha brought up the subject with her dad and Beth after dinner that night. After clearing her plate, Cindy had disappeared up to her room.

"Why was she so quiet tonight?" Beth asked. "I thought she'd at least want to talk about her riding lesson."

"Well, I made the mistake of telling her about Saratoga this afternoon, and she realized that we'd all be leaving for a couple of weeks. I think she feels like we'll be abandoning her. Besides, she doesn't even know where she'll be a month from now."

Beth turned to Samantha's dad and shook her head. "This has got to stop," she said. "Cindy will never have any stability in her life until we get this settled."

Mr. McLean drummed his fingers on the table. "I've appeared in the courtroom twice and told them that we'd like Cindy to stay with us. They've had several people out here checking out the place. They've seen for themselves that it's a good place for a child.

Cindy's told them that she'd rather stay here than go back to the Hadleys'. What more do they want?"

Unfortunately, the next day they found out what the child protection agency had in mind. The phone rang in the stable just as the morning workouts were ending. Mr. McLean had taken the call in the training office, and when he emerged, his face was lined with worry.

"What is it, Dad?" Samantha asked.

"They've found a licensed home for Cindy. Seems a two-parent family has just become available. The caseworker feels Cindy would be better off there. They're planning to come collect her sometime next week."

"No! They can't do that. We have to stop them." Samantha was horrified. She felt her face heat up with anger. Cindy leave Whitebrook? Leave the only warm family she'd ever known? And what about her beloved orphans? And Shining? Samantha was sure it would break Cindy's heart.

She told Ashleigh and Mike the news that afternoon.

"It's all so idiotic!" Samantha cried. "She ran away because she was mistreated at the last foster home they found for her. She's much happier and is getting much better care here!"

"She is happy here," Ashleigh said gently. "But we don't know this new couple. Maybe they'll be nice. It might be hard to accept, and we'd miss Cindy a lot, but maybe the new home could still be good for her."

"I know what you're trying to say," Samantha said unhappily. "But I just don't think it could be as good a home as here."

Samantha was still fuming when she came up to the cottage that evening for dinner. Though no one brought up Cindy's situation at the table, it was plain that Mr. McLean must have had a talk with Cindy. She was withdrawn and had the same mistrustful look she'd had when she'd first come to Whitebrook. She hardly ate a thing. Samantha and Beth tried to talk about light subjects, but Cindy didn't say a word. Samantha felt her heart ache with heaviness. It was all such a waste.

The next few days were drawn out and depressing. Samantha went about her stable chores with a heavy heart. Her mood lifted only slightly when Shining put in a couple of great morning workouts. This was a good sign for the Saratoga race, but it wouldn't seem the same if Cindy wasn't there.

"I've invited a few people over for dinner tonight," Samantha's dad said to her as they walked toward the training barn later that week.

"Great," Samantha said immediately, eager for anything to take her mind away from Cindy's sad situation. "What's the occasion?"

Mr. McLean shrugged and checked a clipboard hanging on the wall. "We need to lighten up the mood around this place, that's all."

When Samantha finished up her evening chores, she headed to the cottage. Beth was in the kitchen, tossing a salad. Samantha's dad was preparing a stir-fry vegetable dish.

"I didn't know you were planning a big meal," Samantha said. "I would have come in earlier to help."

Beth smiled. "Oh, we didn't know, either," she said lightly. "It just sort of happened."

Samantha washed up and changed into clean jeans. She offered to French-braid Cindy's hair. Cindy agreed and stood watching herself in the mirror, her eyes big.

"Thanks," she said. "I've never worn it like that. It looks just like a hunter's tail now, doesn't it?"

Samantha nodded and gave Cindy an impulsive hug.

Ashleigh and Mike arrived at six o'clock, followed by Gene Reese, then Len. The dinner conversation was lively and full of horse talk. Cindy listened intently, and once or twice ventured a question about a couple of the upcoming races and Whitebrook's prospects. When the table was cleared and the guests were served coffee, Mr. McLean and Beth stood up. The couple exchanged looks, then Mr. McLean put his arm around Beth.

"We have an announcement to make," he said as he looked at Samantha, then back at Beth. "Beth and I have been talking, and we've decided to get married."

Samantha felt her cheeks flush. Sure, in the last few months she could see how close her father and Beth had become, but marriage? Yet as the words settled in, she realized how good they sounded. It was right. Her dad and Beth belonged together. It had been so long since she'd considered Beth an intruder in their lives. Now it was as if she'd been part of their lives forever. She was surprised at how much she liked the idea of having a stepmother. Samantha jumped up and caught her dad and Beth both in a big bear hug.

"I'm so happy for you!" she cried.

Beth's eyes grew misty. "Thank you," she said. "It means a lot to me to hear you say that."

"So when's the big day?" Ashleigh asked.

Samantha's dad's eyes twinkled. "Soon. About two weeks. Right before we leave for Saratoga."

"All right!" Ashleigh and Mike chorused.

"It will be a quiet ceremony in Lexington," Beth explained. "We haven't worked out too many details yet, but I have a few plans."

"This is so exciting!" Samantha said. "Whatever help you need, just let me know."

Beth smiled warmly. "Thank you. I could use some

107

help. There's a lot to get done in a short time."

Cindy stood up and hugged Beth and Mr. McLean. Then she slipped out of the room while everyone continued to congratulate the happy couple. Samantha watched Cindy leave, and the gears in her brain started turning.

Later, when the last of the guests had left, Samantha sat with her dad and Beth in the living room. "So," she said, trying to sound casual. "Did Cindy's situation have anything to do with your decision?"

Beth placed her hand on Mr. McLean's shoulder. "Well," she said, "we had been planning to get married at Christmas. It merely helped us decide to move up the date."

"Maybe we'll have more luck with the child welfare people as a married couple," Mr. McLean added. "I'll give them a call tomorrow and see if this will help convince them to let Cindy remain here."

Samantha felt a rush of relief. Maybe this would be the final hurdle in the battle to keep Cindy.

"Amazing!" Mr. McLean said hotly after he'd hung up the phone the next morning. "I told Mrs. Lovell that Beth and I had set a wedding date, and she said that she couldn't promise anything."

Samantha was too stunned to respond. "I told her to talk to my lawyer, that next week is too soon to take Cindy to the new home," Mr. McLean continued. "We need more time to try to resolve this mess."

The next day Samantha drove over to Townsend Acres with Ashleigh for a much-needed distraction. They were going to watch Townsend Princess work. The filly came out on the track and appeared to breeze well, showing no sign of her old injury. Samantha could tell the exercise rider had his hands full holding Princess back, however. She really wanted to stretch out.

"She's coming along nicely," Ken Maddock said, coming up behind the two young women. "I don't want to push her too hard or too fast after her injury, but she's eager and seems to be enjoying herself."

"Do you think she might have some of her mother's talent?" Samantha asked.

Maddock smiled. "Oh, I think she just might."

"Brad and Lavinia haven't been interfering with her training, have they?" Ashleigh asked the trainer.

"Not on your life," Maddock said. "I've talked to Clay Townsend, and he agrees that any training decisions will be made by the three of us."

"Let's hope it stays that way," Ashleigh said.

The rider brought Princess off the training oval. They all walked over as he dismounted.

"You looked great, girl," Ashleigh said to the filly as Maddock checked her over. Her forelegs were wrapped in protective bandages, but as Maddock unwrapped them and felt her previously injured leg, he smiled in satisfaction.

Samantha glanced over to the oval as Her Majesty was ridden out for her work. Brad was at the rail. Thankfully, there was no sign of Lavinia.

"Might as well stay and watch her work," Maddock said of Her Majesty as Hank led Princess off. "She's been burning up the training oval in her workouts since she lost to your filly," he said to Samantha.

Leaning up against the rail, Samantha watched the rider urge the filly out. Samantha felt her stomach sink as Her Majesty effortlessly breezed out a quarter in a shade under twenty-three seconds.

"Don't worry," Ashleigh said to Samantha. "Shining can hold her own. Her works have been impressive, too."

Samantha nodded, but she would have felt better if Lavinia's filly hadn't seemed quite so sharp.

9

ON SATURDAY, SAMANTHA TOOK CINDY OUT RIDING AGAIN. This time she put Shining on the end of a longe line.

"For now, forget about making Shining stop and go, and concentrate only on balancing yourself in your seat," Samantha told Cindy.

She had Cindy knot the reins and cross her arms in front of her. Cindy was hesitant at first, but after a while she relaxed.

"I don't need to hold the reins to hang on," she said happily.

"No, you don't," Samantha said. "Your seat is where you get your security. Now, let's take this idea one step further. Kick your feet out of the stirrups, and cross the leathers over your saddle so they don't bang against Shining's sides."

After the session was over, Samantha said, "You

know, Cindy, you really do have a natural seat. Normally a rider would have to have a few more lessons before I'd feel comfortable putting her on a longe line without reins and stirrups the way I did with you."

Cindy's face lit up. "You really think so?"

"I know so. You have a lot of potential."

"Len said I could help lead the orphans around the paddock today."

"Terrific! I know he really appreciates your help. Hey, I have an idea. How about if we call Tor and ask him if he can squeeze in a lesson? You'd get a chance to hear another perspective, and ride a different horse besides Shining."

"I don't think I could ride another horse besides Shining."

"Well, first of all, I won't be able to give you lessons on Shining anymore, since I'm putting her into heavy training for her next race. And second, a good rider has to learn to ride many horses, not just one. Tor's got some excellent school horses at his stable," Samantha said.

Cindy considered it for a moment. "Okay. Tor's nice."

Samantha walked to the office and called Tor.

"I know you're busy getting ready for the Virginia show, but if you could manage to work in a lesson for Cindy, I think she'd really like it," she explained.

"I just had a private lesson cancel. Bring her over tomorrow," came Tor's answer.

Samantha thanked him and hung up, then found Cindy. "We're on. Tomorrow morning."

"All right!" Cindy said.

The next morning she was up at dawn, dressed in her riding clothes. After the morning workouts and chores were done, Samantha drove her to Tor's stable. She was pleased to see how eager Cindy was. It had been hard over the last few days to watch her mope around Whitebrook.

"Tor has a lot of students who ride on the hunter-jumper circuit," Samantha said as they drove along. "You've met my friend Yvonne. He helped train her and her horse, Cisco. They won a ribbon at the National Horse Show against some pretty serious competition."

"Mandy wants to ride jumpers, too," Cindy said.

Samantha nodded as she turned the car into Tor's driveway. She didn't say anything to Cindy, but she knew the chances of Mandy becoming a great jump rider were slim. The determined young girl might never recover full use of her legs, which she would need to jump well over difficult obstacles. Few other children with a similar physical disability dared to have Mandy's dreams and hopes. Then again, Samantha thought, Mandy had the kind of spunk and strong will that could overcome

113

the most daunting odds to make her dream come true.

Tor was waiting for them at the crossties. He'd already saddled a small, stocky mare.

"Her name's Cinnamon," Tor told Cindy.

Cindy nodded and led the horse to the large indoor ring where Tor conducted many of the lessons. Tor gave Cindy a leg up into the well-worn schooling saddle.

"Thanks for doing this," Samantha said after Cindy had adjusted her stirrups and urged Cinnamon forward at a walk.

Never taking his eyes off Cindy, Tor nodded. "Anytime. By the way, how are things at Whitebrook?"

"Frustrating," Samantha said quietly. "Apart from the good news of the engagement, things aren't really moving along quickly enough in the Cindy department. I just wish they'd decide to let her stay so we could all stop worrying."

"Mmmm," Tor said. "All right, Cindy. Now take up a little of the slack in the rein. Cinnamon thinks she can let her head hang low and amble along. Let her know you expect a solid working walk."

Samantha could see Cindy bite her lip as she focused on Tor's instructions. She sat stiffly in the saddle. But slowly, with Tor's constant encouragement and reassurance, she began to look more comfortable.

"So, how are you feeling about your dad's upcoming marriage?" Tor asked Samantha as Cindy continued around the ring.

"I couldn't be happier."

"I'm glad."

Samantha watched the lesson for a while longer, then decided it might be better if she left Tor to work with Cindy without interruption. She wandered over to the barn and made her way to where Yvonne's horse, Cisco, was stabled. She scratched the big Thoroughbred under his jaw for a minute, then wandered down the aisle to look at the other horses. In one of the stalls she noticed Angelique Dubret's beautiful warmblood. The tall blond girl Samantha had seen at the Pony Commandos' lesson was in the stall, adjusting the horse's blanket.

"Hi," Samantha said.

The girl turned. Up close, Samantha noticed, she was even prettier than she'd seemed at a distance. "Hello," Angelique said coolly.

"Beautiful horse."

The girl's eyes flicked over Samantha. "Thanks. His name's Appraiser."

"Well, see you around," Samantha said when it became clear that Angelique didn't really want her there. She returned to the ring just as Tor was finishing up the lesson. Cindy had a big smile on her face. Samantha didn't think she'd ever seen her look better than she did right now, with her flushed cheeks, shining eyes, and wisps of thin blond hair escaping from under her dusty hunt cap.

"We trotted a lot, and Tor even let me canter," she said proudly. "Cinnamon's a nice horse."

"That's great," Samantha said, reaching out to pat Cinnamon.

After Cindy disappeared to walk and groom Cinnamon, Samantha walked with Tor to the office.

"Thanks for working with her," she said sincerely. "She seems so happy, and with the way things have been going for her, it really helps."

"It didn't make any difference to the authorities that your dad and Beth are getting married?" Tor asked as he turned to check his schedule board on the wall.

Samantha frowned. "They agreed not to take her immediately to that one home they were talking about, but they still wouldn't make any promises."

"This sure has dragged on a long time." Then, changing the subject, he talked to Samantha about the upcoming schedule for the Pony Commandos. "I've got to step up my training with Top Hat," he said. "Our show is just around the corner."

"Tell you what," Samantha said. "Yvonne and Gregg and I can handle the Pony Commandos this week, so you can concentrate on your work."

"Thanks," Tor said. "I hate to miss a session, but

there's a lot to be done. You might have to do without Yvonne as well. She and Cisco need some extra work right now, too."

"I think I'll ask Cindy to come help with me," Samantha said. "It will do her some good to see other riders who are starting out."

"Good idea," Tor said. He looked up as the door opened and Angelique stepped inside the office. She seemed surprised to see Samantha there and gave her a cool look.

"Oh, Samantha, this is Angelique Dubret," he said. "Angelique, Samantha McLean."

Samantha nodded. "Hi. We met, sort of."

Angelique gave the smallest of nods to Samantha, then turned to Tor. "I need your advice on something if you have a few minutes before your next lesson," she said with a smile directed only to Tor.

"Sure," Tor began.

Samantha interrupted quickly. "Well, I've got to get going. I'll see you tonight."

"Oh, Sammy, I forgot to tell you. I'll be a little late. Angelique and I are going to work with Appraiser and Top Hat after my last class. The Virginia show is coming up soon. I'll give you a call later."

"Fine," Samantha said, feeling anything but fine. She suddenly felt like an outsider, especially when she saw Angelique's satisfied smile. She didn't know what to make of the twinge of jealousy she felt.

Turning, she hurried out of the office, telling herself she was imagining things.

The afternoon was hot and sticky when the Pony Commandos assembled in one of the outdoor rings the next day at Tor's stable. Samantha had set up two low jumps. Several of the Pony Commandos took turns trotting their ponies over the low fences, and Samantha was pleased to see how well they did. While Janet, Gregg, and Mrs. Jarvis took them off for their water break, Cindy asked Samantha if she'd ever be able to jump.

Samantha smiled at the girl. "You bet," she said. "Let's schedule another lesson on Cinnamon, and we'll work our way toward that goal."

Mandy came up just then, expertly maneuvering Butterball between Samantha and Cindy. "Can we jump that?" she asked Samantha, pointing to a brush jump in the corner of the ring that was set higher on the standards than the others. "Butterball wants to jump higher."

Samantha patted Butterball's nose and regarded Mandy. "Let's take it one step at a time," Samantha said. "Butterball needs to learn a few more things at these lower heights before we move up."

Mandy seemed to accept the answer, and nudged the fat pony with her thin legs to rejoin her classmates.

"She really loves to ride, doesn't she?" Cindy said, her gaze following the small girl. "And she doesn't let anything stop her. She doesn't feel sorry for herself or anything."

Samantha looked fondly at Mandy. "No, she doesn't."

Cindy stood outside the ring and watched Samantha work the Commandos over a few more jumps. Suddenly she let out a yell. "Mandy's headed toward the brush jump!" she cried.

"Mandy, stop!" Samantha called.

But the little girl hung on tightly as Butterball folded his short legs and made a valiant attempt to clear the high fence. Cindy covered her face with her hands as Butterball fell back, unable to clear the top, sending Mandy out of the saddle into the dirt. The riderless horse trotted across the ring in confusion, his reins dangling. Samantha rushed over to Mandy while Cindy darted after Butterball. Mrs. Jarvis sat with a stricken expression outside the ring, clearly wanting to rush to her daughter but not wanting to upset her any further.

"Mandy, are you hurt?" Samantha asked anxiously, kneeling down in the dirt to inspect the little girl's arms and legs.

Mandy's face was streaked with grime, and she wiped her mouth with her gloved hand and shook her head. Gingerly she sat up. She looked devastated and embarrassed. "I messed up," she said weakly. "I should have given him a little more rein. How could I have been so dumb?"

"You and Butterball just haven't had enough experience to be trying jumps that high," Samantha told the girl firmly.

Cindy led Butterball over, and Samantha helped Mandy to her feet, carefully checking again to make sure she hadn't hurt herself in any way. "Come on," Samantha said encouragingly. "Let's get you back in the saddle."

Mandy hesitated.

"You know we never end a lesson on a bad note," Samantha added. "The only thing to do after a spill is to get right back in the saddle."

"Yes, I know," Mandy said, looking down at her feet, but she took a few awkward steps to Butterball's side.

After Samantha helped Mandy remount, she told her not to try the more difficult jumps without permission and supervision. Mandy nodded, but she was obviously feeling guilty. The rest of the lesson proceeded without any further problems.

When it was over, Samantha spotted Tor in the next ring taking Top Hat around a course. Anqelique was standing in the center of the ring, and Samantha noticed how cool and elegant she looked, even in the heat and humidity. She was conscious that she herself was sweaty and dirty, and that her damp hair was plastered to her forehead. She was horrified to realize that she was truly feeling jealous, especially as Tor rode up to the girl after one of his jumps and the two talked for a moment before he moved off again.

"Come on, you guys," Samantha said. "Let's watch Tor and see how he puts some of the things we're learning into practice."

The Commandos lined up at the rail and watched as, smoothly and effortlessly, Tor pointed the big white Thoroughbred at fence after fence. First the brick wall, then a large oxer, and over to a big triple combination.

Samantha gazed at Angelique, who was watching Tor intently, and felt herself being looked over critically in return. Samantha didn't like the feeling.

"Wow," Cindy breathed. "Did you see the way Tor did that?"

Samantha turned her gaze back to Tor and Top Hat. "See how Tor uses his weight to communicate to his horse?" Samantha told the Commandos. She glanced at Mandy, who was studying Tor and Top Hat, too. "This is what we were working on in our lesson over the lower jumps."

The Commandos stayed for a while before heading to the stable to untack their ponies. Samantha was just walking toward the tack room with an armload of bridles when she heard several loud sobs. Hurriedly she went around the corner and saw Mandy leaning against the stable wall, crying bitterly.

"Mandy, what's wrong?" Samantha said, rushing over. "Were you hurt after all?"

Fiercely Mandy shook her head and lifted her dirt-stained face. "No," she wept. "It's just that I'll never be able to jump like Tor and Yvonne. I can't even make it over a stupid little brush jump. I hate being like this. It's not fair. I'll never be like everybody else."

"That's simply not true."

"It is," Mandy insisted. "Everyone's lying to me. I'm not going to ride in the show. What's the use?"

She pulled away from Samantha and started walking clumsily toward the car. Samantha headed over to where Mrs. Jarvis was waiting in the stable office and quickly explained what had happened.

"She gets her hopes up too high," Mrs. Jarvis said sadly. "But her father and I will talk to her. I'm sure she'll get over it. I can't believe she'd actually skip the show. It's all she's been talking about."

Later Samantha pulled Tor aside and told him about the problem, but he didn't appear to be that concerned.

"It was bound to upset her," he said. "But I'm sure she'll get over it in a hurry."

He patted Samantha on the shoulder. "Listen, I've gotta go. One of my riders is waiting for me."

Stung, Samantha pulled back. This wasn't like Tor. Normally he was so concerned about the welfare of the disabled children, especially Mandy. She watched as he walked toward Angelique, who was leading her beautiful blood-bay warmblood toward his stall.

Yvonne came up beside Samantha.

"So what do you think of Angelique?" Yvonne asked, following Samantha's gaze.

"I don't know," Samantha said. She watched Tor lead Angelique into the ring, their blond heads bent close together in what looked like an intimate conversation. *Don't be silly*, Samantha told herself sternly. *Angelique has nothing to do with Tor's mood. He's just got a lot on his mind, that's all. He's got to concentrate on getting his students ready for the big shows.* But for some reason, she couldn't exactly convince herself that it was true.

"She's an incredible rider," Yvonne added. "She told one of the other private boarders that she's known Tor for ages and has competed in a lot of the same shows he has."

That news didn't make Samantha feel any better, but she didn't say anything to Yvonne about her troubled thoughts.

The next morning Samantha drove into Lexington with her dad, Beth, and Cindy. They stopped off first at the child protection offices. Samantha waited in an uncomfortable plastic chair in a waiting room while the rest of the group went into one of the offices. When Cindy emerged a while later, she was smiling.

"I think they're going to let me stay," she announced excitedly.

"No promises," Mr. McLean said as they got into the car. "Mrs. Lovell says it helps that we're getting married, but nothing's definite yet."

While they were in town, they went shopping for a wedding dress for Beth, then looked over sample flower arrangements. Samantha agreed with Beth that simple white roses would look elegant and cool at a summer wedding. Afterward they stopped at Yogurt Blues for frozen yogurt.

That evening Samantha called Tor to tell him the good news about Cindy and to fill him in on the wedding plans. Once again he seemed incredibly distracted. He barely expressed excitement over the fact that Cindy would be staying at Whitebrook.

Instead he talked briefly about Top Hat, then mentioned his hopes for some of his students. Just before they hung up, he said, "Hey, Sammy, about that movie date we'd planned for tomorrow—do you mind taking a rain check? Angelique needs some extra work, and I've scheduled a couple of extra sessions for her."

Samantha heard herself say, "Sure, no problem," but she was horrified to feel a nasty pang of jealousy.

After she hung up, she wandered down to the barn to check on Shining.

"I am being ridiculous. I know it," she told her horse as she adjusted her blanket. "Tor's never given me any reason to doubt his loyalty."

Shining whuffed loudly and nodded her lovely head as if in agreement.

"Still," Samantha went on in a worried voice, "it isn't like Tor to hurry me off the phone and break dates."

She rubbed Shining's silky mane and sighed.

10

THOUGH HER FATHER AND BETH'S WEDDING WAS TO BE A small affair, Samantha was surprised at how much there was to arrange. She made several confirming calls to the church, the florist, and the soloist who was to sing at the service. She helped find a new photographer when the first one who had been hired had to cancel at the last minute, and she patched up a mix-up over the cake order.

Samantha took another trip into Lexington with Beth and Cindy. After picking up Beth's dress, they headed to the junior shop, where they spent several hours shopping for new clothes for Cindy. Afterward they took her to a hair-cutting salon, where the stylist trimmed her shoulder-length hair in a becoming blunt cut.

"That was fun," Cindy declared shyly, clutching her shopping bags.

"I like your new cut," Beth said. "It frames your face and brings out your eyes. You look very pretty."

Samantha saw Cindy flush with pleasure.

That evening after dinner, Samantha went to the barn to visit Shining. Her life was about to change in a big way, and she wanted to share her thoughts with her beloved horse. She sat for a long while, running her hands over Shining's smooth neck and listening to the familiar sounds of contented horses settling down for the night. Everything would be fine, she told herself. Cindy would stay with them, Mandy would snap out of her funk, and nothing was going on between Tor and Angelique.

The day of the wedding dawned clear and warm. Little wisps of clouds chased through the sky as Tor, Samantha, and Cindy followed Mike, Ashleigh, and Mr. Reese over the country roads to Lexington. Samantha's dad and Beth had driven on ahead. Tor seemed his old self, talking about Shining and his horses and asking about Mandy. He talked easily with Cindy as well, and Samantha smiled in relief. She'd been silly to think that there was anything to worry about with Angelique. He didn't mention her name once when he talked about his students and the shows that were coming up. Samantha relaxed, and once they arrived at the little chapel, she and Janet helped Beth with the last-minute preparations.

When Beth was ready, Samantha slipped onto a bench next to Tor. "This is it," she whispered in his ear, reaching over to take his hand.

She listened to the soft classical music filling the chapel and admired the perfume of the white roses in the decorative stands by the altar. Her thoughts drifted to her mother, and somehow Samantha knew that she would have wanted everyone to move on with their lives. Sunshine streamed through the stained-glass windows, and Samantha could hear the soft whispers of the wedding guests. Beth looked spectacular as she came down the aisle in her light, vintage lace tea-length dress, and her dad looked handsome in his smart summer-weight suit. Soft strains of music filled the air as Beth and her father were pronounced husband and wife. Tears filled Samantha's eyes, and she jumped up from her seat to hug the happy couple. The laughing group headed to a quaint restaurant in town for dinner.

"It's nice to see your dad so happy," Tor said as they drove home after dinner.

Samantha leaned against his shoulder and nodded. Her dad had been through so much ever since her mom had died, and he deserved to find happiness again.

"And Cindy seems much happier these days, too."

A small frown creased Samantha's brow. "I know. I only wish my dad and Beth would be given the okay to be Cindy's foster parents once and for all."

"Well, let's hope the authorities will really take a close look at Cindy's case," Tor said. "I'm sure they see how determined your dad and Beth are and how well Cindy is doing here. That's probably why Cindy's been allowed to stay at Whitebrook as long as she has."

Samantha didn't respond. For now she just wanted to enjoy being with Tor.

In the days following the wedding, as they made preparations for Saratoga, Samantha was up extra early each morning to avoid the heat and humidity of the late July days. She worked intently with Shining, keeping her in top shape with slow, stamina-building gallops on the oval. In the late afternoons, after the humidity and heat let up somewhat, she saddled up a retired racehorse that belonged to Mike named Saturday Flyer and continued giving Cindy lessons. Flyer was quiet and dependable, but his trot wasn't as smooth as Shining's, and Cindy really had to work to ride him well. Still, she hung on determinedly, and Samantha was happy with her progress.

When Cindy trotted without stirrups for the first time, her face lit up as she found the posting motion and was able to trot rhythmically twice around the big ring.

"I did it!" she exclaimed, pulling to a stop in front of Samantha.

"You sure did," Samantha said. "Flyer's doing the best he can, but when you ride Shining again, you'll get a chance to feel what a smooth trot is like."

Cindy nodded. "I can't wait. I miss riding Shining."

Her smile faded, and Samantha wondered if it had to do with the fact that Saratoga was fast approaching. No one really wanted to speculate on whether or not Cindy would be able to make the trip.

On the way back to the barn Samantha thought about how much Cindy had improved in her few short lessons. It was satisfying to watch a rider make so much progress. Tor had explained to her how great it felt when one of his students did well, but she had never really understood until now. That thought reminded her that she had barely heard from Tor since the wedding. She knew how busy he was preparing for the Virginia show, but she couldn't help feeling that something was wrong.

The following morning Samantha took Cindy with her to Tor's stable for the Pony Commandos' lesson. Their big show was two weeks from Wednesday. Five of the Commandos were grooming their ponies under Yvonne and Gregg's watchful eye, but Samantha noticed immediately that Mandy wasn't with them. She spotted Tor standing near the office, talking to Angelique.

"What's wrong with Mandy?" Cindy whispered, pointing to the Jarvises' car. Mandy was sitting in the backseat, her arms crossed stubbornly in front of her.

Samantha hurried over to Mandy.

"Is everything okay?" she asked with concern.

Mr. Jarvis looked tired. Mandy's jaw was set. She looked away when Samantha approached.

"Mandy doesn't feel well this afternoon," he said wearily. "Are you sure you don't feel well enough to ride?"

Mandy shook her head, her mop of dark curls swinging around her face. "My head aches, and my— my throat is sore," she said, still not looking at Samantha.

"Well, in that case, Mandy," Samantha said, "I guess you should just go home and rest. When you're feeling better, Yvonne or I will give you an extra lesson so you're ready for the show. In the meantime you can come over to Whitebrook to visit Shining."

Mandy nodded but kept her eyes lowered. Then she and her father drove away.

"Mandy really has herself worked up about that spill," Samantha said in a discouraged voice to Tor after the lesson was over.

"Just give her time," Tor said. "She'll come around."

He glanced at some schedules he was carrying and frowned, tapping a pencil against his clipboard. "By the way, Sammy, speaking of time, I'm really sorry, but I just don't see how I can make Sierra's training session tomorrow. Can you manage the session on your own? I'm taking Angelique to a schooling show. She really needs the extra work before we leave for Virginia the weekend after this."

Samantha felt a stab of jealousy and disappointment well up in her throat. "Sure, no problem," she said, a little too brightly.

"Thanks. I knew you'd understand. I'll be there for the next one."

Samantha drove home in silence, hardly noticing how talkative Cindy was in the car. She went on and on about the Pony Commandos' upcoming show. She seemed as excited as if she were entering it herself.

"Are you feeling okay?" Cindy finally asked Samantha as they pulled into the driveway in front of the McLean cottage.

Samantha turned to face her. "Yeah. Sorry. I was just thinking about what I should do about Mandy."

"It seemed like a good idea to ask her to come visit Shining," Cindy said thoughtfully. "It'll help her remember how much she loves horses and why she wants to ride so much."

Samantha climbed out of the car. "I think you're right."

Mandy came over the next afternoon. And although it seemed to Samantha that she enjoyed just being with Shining and watching Samantha take

Sierra over several hurdles, she didn't mention the Pony Commandos or their show.

"So are you excited about the show?" Samantha heard Cindy ask her.

Mandy paused, then said, "I don't know."

"You are a good rider, you know," Cindy added quietly.

Mandy shook her head. "No, I'm not. You saw me fall."

"You just didn't have enough experience to jump that high. But you won't get better if you don't ride some more," Cindy pointed out.

"I'll never be as good as Tor and Yvonne," Mandy said flatly. "I was dumb to think I could be."

Samantha began to worry when Mandy didn't show up for the special lesson she'd arranged. The Commandos' show was in a few days. She found Tor in the indoor ring and told him that Mandy had missed her lesson. He seemed distracted and dismissed her worries. But when Angelique entered the ring on Appraiser, he gave her his full attention.

Samantha hung around for a few minutes and watched Angelique's lesson. She admired the powerful way that Appraiser jumped. The big, muscular horse really used his hindquarters and stayed balanced throughout the difficult course Tor had set up. Samantha had to admit that Angelique was an excellent rider. But did she have to stand so close to Tor when he

133

gave her instructions? Samantha found herself fuming as she drove back to Whitebrook. That evening she phoned Mandy's house, and Mandy agreed to come to the stable for some makeup lessons on Butterball.

Cindy sat on the rail as Samantha worked with Mandy the next afternoon. "Mandy seems to be getting her nerve back," Cindy said afterward to Samantha.

"But not her enthusiasm," Samantha responded, biting her lip.

The lesson went well, but Mandy refused to jump. While they groomed Butterball, Samantha took a deep breath and brought up the subject of the show, but Mandy stubbornly refused to talk about it.

Nothing happened over the next few days to lighten Samantha's mood. She and Yvonne agreed to add on an extra lesson for the Pony Commandos to get them ready for the show, but Mandy was still quiet and unenthusiastic. Samantha was beginning to miss Tor as well. When she saw him, he seemed tense and withdrawn. Angelique seemed to follow Tor everywhere, and Samantha could hardly talk to him without Angelique turning up at just the wrong moment.

Samantha's mood was temporarily lifted when Maureen called and invited her to a swimming party for all of their friends on Thursday night, but when she called Tor, he told her he wouldn't be able to make it.

"I'd like to go," he said. "But I've decided to leave for Virginia on Thursday afternoon, and there's still a lot to get done."

Samantha twisted the cord of the phone and tried to stuff down the thought that Angelique would be with him. "I thought you weren't going until Friday."

"I know, Sammy. But like I said, I changed my plans. It's been a crazy time," Tor went on. "I probably won't even be able to make it up to Saratoga, except for one or two days to ride Sierra in his 'chases."

"I understand," Samantha said quietly, trying to be a good sport. "Well, good luck at your show. I know you and Top Hat will do well."

That night Samantha sat in Shining's stall, trying to reassure herself that after the pressure let up, everything would be okay with Tor again. But she felt a wave of sadness swirl around her. Instead of being one of the best summers of her life, this was turning out to be one of the worst.

Shining whuffed softly, and Samantha tried to comfort herself with her beloved horse's presence. At least she could concentrate on getting Shining ready for her race at Saratoga.

11

ON SUNDAY EVENING AFTER EVERYONE HAD GONE TO BED, Samantha lay awake, staring at her ceiling. She hadn't heard a word from Tor about how the show had gone. She knew he was busy, but he'd been busy at shows before and had always taken the time to at least make a quick phone call.

What if something had happened? The thought made her toss and turn for most of the night. At four thirty, shortly before she'd normally be up to work the horses, she got out of bed. She couldn't stop thinking that something terrible had happened to Tor. Why else wouldn't he have called her? She quickly threw on some clothes and slipped out into the semi-darkness to her father's car. Soon she was on the road, heading toward Tor's stable.

As she pulled into the driveway her headlights

shone on the Nelsons' van in the yard. So he was home, Samantha thought. She hopped out of the car and made her way to the stable, where she saw Tor bent over, unwrapping Top Hat's shipping boots. She noticed a bandage around one of the horse's forelegs. When Tor looked up, Samantha saw his eyes were rimmed with red.

"Sammy," he said with surprise. "What are you doing here?"

"Is everything okay? When I didn't hear from you after the show, I got worried."

"Well, no one was hurt too badly, and we're all home safe and sound."

"What happened?"

Tor led Top Hat into his stall. "Don't ask," he groaned. "The van broke down, and it took me forever to figure out how to fix it. We sat by the side of the road all night doing the repair. We just got home."

"Oh, no," Samantha said. "And what happened to Top Hat's leg?"

"Right after we finished competing, we came around a slippery corner by the temporary stalls. Top Hat lost his footing and ended up going down. It was lucky that all he got was the gash on his cannon. It should heal quickly."

Just then, Samantha saw Angelique coming down the aisle, not a hair out of place.

"Here's that cream I told you about, Tor," she

said, looking Samantha over. "Oh, hi."

Angelique handed the cream to Tor and started explaining how well it had worked on Appraiser, as if Samantha weren't even there. It was like . . . she owned Tor. "Is there anything I can do to help you?" Angelique almost purred, looking at him intently.

"You're as tired as I am," Tor responded.

"You need the help," Angelique answered. "I'll get the tack and our ribbons from the van, and I needed to ask you about—"

She dropped her voice slightly, so that Samantha couldn't quite hear what she was saying.

"Listen, I have to get back to Whitebrook," she said quickly. "I haven't worked Shining yet, and I promised I'd take Rocky Heights out for a gallop and—" She felt like she was babbling, and she stopped midsentence.

"See you later," Tor said lightly.

Samantha spun on her heels, jumped into the car, and hurried away from the stable. She felt like she'd been kicked. Now it was clear. Tor had fallen for Angelique. *Well, how could he not?* she asked herself miserably. Angelique was gorgeous and sophisticated and could stay up all night helping fix a van and still look fresh in the morning. Samantha looked down at her rumpled stable clothes and sighed. It wasn't until she pulled into Whitebrook's driveway that she realized she hadn't even asked Tor how he and Top Hat had done.

When Samantha got to the cottage, everyone was already up and out. She went to the stable and saw that Cindy had tacked up Shining.

"Oh, there you are," Cindy said. "I got her ready for you."

Samantha managed a smile. Automatically she checked everything over, ensuring that there were no twisted straps, that the snaffle bit was resting comfortably in Shining's mouth, and that the saddle was placed in the correct spot over Shining's withers. Cindy had done a great job. Shining had been groomed meticulously, and her light racing saddle and bridle were adjusted precisely. "Thanks," she said.

"While you're working her, I'll get Rocky ready," Cindy said, bounding away.

Samantha led Shining out onto the oval and waited while Ashleigh took Blues King for his gallop. Mike was holding the stopwatch today, and he alternated between watching Blues King and writing notes on a clipboard he was carrying. Mike signaled Samantha when it was her turn. She jammed her helmet on, flipped down her goggles, and set her jaw. The morning was crisp, with no hint yet of the heat Samantha knew would come later. Shining tossed her pretty head, and there was a decided spring in her step as she moved out to the training gates.

"You feel good, don't you, girl?" Samantha asked just before the training gates flew open, and Shining whuffed as if in agreement. The next moment she was off like a shot, thundering down the track. Samantha kneaded her hands along Shining's neck as they swept around the turn. The cool wind stung Samantha's face, and she felt Shining's powerful movement beneath her. She was conscious only of the pounding of hoofbeats and rhythmic snorts of breath. The marker poles flew by, and when Samantha pulled up at last, she knew that once again Shining had put in a great performance.

"Well done," Mike said, looking at his stopwatch and jotting the time on his clipboard.

Samantha rode back, pleased that even though she felt terrible about what had happened with Tor, she hadn't spoiled Shining's workout.

That afternoon Samantha called Yvonne and they agreed to meet over at Tor's stable to talk about the Pony Commandos' show.

"Cindy's going to help us, too," she informed Yvonne.

"Great! We can use all the help we can get," Yvonne exclaimed before hanging up.

Samantha was relieved that Cindy was so enthusiastic about helping. She herself was in no mood to even think about the show. All she could think about was that she'd be seeing Tor. Maybe he'd come rushing over and explain to her that things weren't really the way they'd seemed last night.

But when they arrived at the stable, Tor was off in

the outer ring with Angelique. Samantha watched them from a distance for a few minutes, noting that it certainly wasn't evident that Angelique had been up all night. She was riding one of Tor's father's school horses flawlessly, taking jump after jump. Samantha was surprised that Angelique would be riding at all. She'd have thought the girl would take a day off after a big show.

She shook her head and went to the crossties, where Yvonne was bathing Cisco.

"Tor said to tell you we should carry on without him," Yvonne called as she carefully rinsed out Cisco's coat. "He says he's got the jumping course designed. He asked if we'd come up with lunch plans and trophy ideas."

"Fine," Samantha muttered. Then she realized that she'd better try to be a good sport. After all, she didn't want to bring Yvonne and Cindy down. Still, she had a hard time concentrating, and after half an hour, it was clear they weren't getting anywhere. Finally Yvonne said, "We're not making much progress. How about if we meet here again tomorrow?" She looked closely at Samantha, and Samantha smiled in gratitude at her friend. It was clear Yvonne knew her too well. She was giving her the opportunity to go talk with Tor.

"Sorry," Samantha said. "I've got a lot on my mind."

"Don't worry about it," Yvonne said, flashing a grin. "Hey, Cindy, come with me to the indoor ring.

Tor's dad is trying out a new horse he's thinking of buying. He's supposed to be a top-class jumper. Let's go and see if he lives up to his reputation, shall we?"

"I'd like that," Cindy said, her face lighting up.

"I'll go find Tor and meet you in the yard in a while," Samantha said, checking her watch. Surely Tor and Angelique had finished their lesson by now.

She made her way to the office. The door was open, and she saw that Tor was inside. She was about to poke her head inside and say hello when suddenly she realized that he wasn't alone. Angelique was there, too. The two of them were talking in low voices. Samantha froze as Angelique reached over and laid her hand on Tor's arm. Samantha watched, but Tor didn't pull away. Feeling like she'd just received a blow to her stomach, Samantha took off in a run from the office, slowing only when she approached the indoor ring.

"Come on," she said in a tight voice to Cindy, whose eyes were glued to a big, flea-bitten gray who was crashing into a series of jumps. "We'd better get back. I've got to work Sierra, and we've got loads of chores to do."

All the way home, she was silent. She hardly listened as Cindy rattled on and on about the wild, half-trained gray horse. Samantha kept replaying the scene she'd just witnessed in the office. This was it. Her relationship with Tor was over.

12

"SO INSTEAD OF JUST ONE EXHIBITION, THE SHOW COULD be like a series of classes," Yvonne said to Samantha the next day. They were back at Tor's stable, sitting on hay bales with Cindy, discussing the Pony Commandos' show. Yvonne had just taken a jumping lesson on Cisco. She was hot and sweaty and hadn't even protested when Cindy turned the hose on her as she helped bathe Cisco. "We'll start with a flat class, just the walk, trot, and canter, then move on to a jumping class. We'll ask Tor to design a small figure-eight course made up of low crossrails and some verticals. Nothing too scary."

"And how about a grooming class?" Cindy chimed in. "I could help the kids with brushing and putting ribbons in the horses' manes and tails. Maybe the winner's prize could be a special hoofpick or currycomb or something."

"Great idea!" exclaimed Samantha. "That's how we should start out the morning."

"And Beth and Janet are bringing a picnic lunch."

"I asked Ashleigh to judge, and she said she'll be glad to," Samantha said, happy to have at least come up with one idea.

"Has Mandy changed her mind about showing?" Yvonne asked suddenly.

Samantha shook her head.

Yvonne frowned. "I wish she'd realize that everyone has a few spills now and then. Do you think it would help if Tor called and talked to her? She just idolizes him. He could tell her a few stories about show-jumping spills—and riders who get right back up into the saddle."

Samantha shrugged. She had figured Tor would come over to talk with them and help them set up for the next day's show, but when they'd first arrived at the stable, he'd merely waved in an offhanded way and disappeared down the barn aisle. It was plain to Samantha that he couldn't care less about the show— or whether or not Mandy rode in it. Samantha drew an aimless doodle in the dirt with a riding crop someone had tossed down after a lesson and remembered back to the day when Tor had come up with the idea of the Pony Commandos' show. How long ago that seemed now!

"That sounds fine," Samantha said, wondering

where Angelique was. She hadn't seen her, but that didn't mean she wasn't hanging around talking to Tor, getting advice about Appraiser or something.

"I have another idea," Cindy said, sitting up straight, her eyes sparkling. "How about instead of buying trophies, we take shoes from each of the ponies and paint them silver and gold? We could mount them on a plaque and give one to each child as a prize."

"The kids would love them," Yvonne said.

Samantha nodded. "I love the one you painted for me. I have it hanging right by Shining's Keeneland trophy. It's very special."

Once Samantha and Cindy had driven back to Whitebrook in Samantha's dad's car, Cindy rushed off to make her horseshoes.

Samantha decided to call Mandy. The girl had promised to come to Tor's later that afternoon for a special lesson.

"You know, we're getting closer and closer to the show date," Samantha said over the phone. "Are you sure you won't change your mind?"

Mandy was silent. "I'll be at the stable at five," she said finally.

"I don't understand," Samantha said softly as she helped Mandy into the saddle later that afternoon. Cindy had come with her and was visiting with the horses in the stable block. "You've always wanted to jump, yet you haven't jumped Butterball since the fall, and you won't even consider showing."

Mandy wrinkled her tiny nose. "I still like horses, but I just don't want to show. Everyone else rides better than I do."

"That's not true," Samantha said. "You know you're a good rider."

"And poor Butterball," Mandy wailed. "He must hate having me for a rider. I can't even make him jump right."

"Oh, Mandy, that's simply not the way it is," Samantha started to say. But she felt too overwhelmed to continue trying to convince Mandy that she was all wrong.

"Chin up, heels down," Samantha said mechanically as Mandy started around the ring.

Mandy followed her instructions. Little droplets of sweat gathered around her hunt cap. Samantha could see how stiff she was and how nervous. She'd lost some of the balance and seat she'd acquired over the last few months.

"You're doing fine, now relax," Samantha called.

She pushed her hair out of her face and found her mind wandering. It was harder and harder to concentrate on the lesson. Mandy seemed so wooden, and Samantha felt too depressed to try to relax her and help her be more supple.

"Are you ready to take a jump or two?" Samantha asked after the little girl had had a good workout on the flat.

Mandy shook her head. "Not today."

Samantha wasn't surprised at the answer. Oh, well, if Mandy wasn't going to participate in the show, she wasn't going to push the jumping, Samantha decided. She'd just have to wait for Mandy to regain her confidence on her own.

"Samantha," Mandy said, staring down at her. "Are you mad at me?"

"No, I'm not. Really, I'm not," Samantha said quickly. "If you don't want to jump or ride in the show, that's your decision and it's okay with me." She didn't want Mandy to feel pressured. "Let's get Butterball cooled out now. Cindy can give you a hand. I still have to give Sierra some exercise when I get home."

Mandy turned to Cindy as she came up, taking Butterball's reins.

"How'd your lesson go?" Cindy asked as they walked toward the crossties.

"Fine," Mandy said. Then after a pause she added, "No, not fine. Samantha was . . . funny. I think she's mad at me. She said she wasn't, but I don't believe her."

Cindy helped the little girl dismount, then assisted her as she took off the bridle and placed the halter on

Butterball. "Why would Samantha be mad at you?" she asked.

Mandy's eyes filled, and she brushed at them impatiently. "I think she's mad at me because I won't jump and I won't ride in the show."

Cindy took the saddle off the pony and set it on the rack behind her. "I don't think she's mad, but I know she'd like you to ride. We all would like to see you ride. You're good, and you've worked a lot on your riding," she said quietly. "Just because you had one little spill—"

"I have to go," Mandy said abruptly, and maneuvered herself awkwardly down the aisle. Cindy followed her.

"Mandy, you've got to listen to me," Cindy persisted. "I may not know that much about horses, but I'm learning. And I know you can't give up just because things are tough."

"Leave me alone," Mandy said, her eyes flashing.

But Cindy merely looked back at her and said, "No."

Mandy was startled. "No?" she echoed.

"No," Cindy said. "I won't. I won't give up. I know how much you love horses, and I know how much you want to become a good rider, just like I do. Well, you never will if you don't try. That means practicing jumping and showing. You have to prove to yourself that you can do it."

"But what if I can't?" Mandy sniffled and wiped at her eyes.

"Oh, Mandy, you were doing great until the day you fell. You can only get better if you keep riding. I've only just started, but I know I'm getting better every time I have a lesson. Maybe we could go for a ride together with Samantha sometime."

"That would be fun. I guess you're right. I should ride in the show. Want to come with me to tell Samantha?" Mandy asked.

She took Cindy's hand, and together they went looking for Samantha.

When Samantha saw the two girls coming toward her, each with a big grin on her face, she wondered what on earth was up.

"I've decided to be in the show," Mandy announced. "That is, if it isn't too late."

"All right!" Samantha burst out, relief flowing through her. "No, of course it's not too late. Oh, I'm so glad."

She hugged Mandy and darted a glance at Cindy, who looked ridiculously pleased with herself.

The morning of the show dawned beautiful. Beth left early to help Janet pick up several of the Commandos in the van. After finishing up the stable work, Samantha packed the big lunch Janet and Beth had prepared for the Commandos and placed it in a cooler. Then she and Cindy gathered up other supplies, threw them into the backseat, and drove over to Tor's. Yvonne met them in the parking lot and helped them unload, talking nonstop.

"You should see it," she said as they set the coolers down inside the training office. "Everyone's here, and the Commandos have been grooming their ponies and tying ribbons into their manes. We've gone through yards and yards of ribbon. Some of the ponies might end up bald from being brushed so much."

Samantha managed a grin. "Is Mandy here?" she asked.

"You bet," Yvonne said. "She was one of the first to show up. You'll hardly recognize Butterball. He looks like a real show pony. She's determined to make him beautiful. How did you convince her to ride?"

Samantha glanced at Cindy. "I didn't," she said. "I think Cindy had something to do with her change of heart."

Cindy flushed. "I'd better go help the kids," she said, scurrying off.

Samantha watched her go, then turned to her friend. "Has Tor been around?" she asked.

Yvonne looked away for a moment. "Yeah, he's around. But he hasn't been involved much with us.

He gave me my lesson first thing, and he's been working with Angelique ever since." Seeing Samantha's look, she added quietly, "Don't be too hard on him. He's been really busy with all the shows coming up."

Samantha clenched her teeth, then started to lay out some of the things from the baskets. "Is everything ready?" she asked Yvonne.

"I just have to get the programs from my car. I'll pass them out to the parents as soon as Gregg gets here," she said.

"Cindy stayed up late last night making the horse-show trophies." Samantha lifted them out of one of the baskets.

"They look great. Silver, huh," Yvonne said. "One for each child."

Just then the screen door of the training office banged open, and three excited Pony Commandos burst into the office. Eight-year-old Timmy immediately wheeled his wheelchair right up to the cooler.

"Yum, look at all the food!" he exclaimed.

"Where are the trophies?" demanded little Charmaine Green. "Can I see them?" she asked, poking her strawberry-blond head into one of the baskets, then spotting the shining horseshoe plaques on the table.

"Let me see," the other Pony Commandos clamored.

Yvonne laughed and held up her hand. "Come on,

guys. Let's get out of here and saddle the ponies. We need to warm up and get started."

"There you are," Gregg said as he came into the office and viewed the preparations. "Follow me, Commandos."

Forty-five minutes later six spruced-up children dressed in a colorful array of riding clothes, both borrowed and bought, lined up in the ring with their ponies.

Their parents cheered as they started around the neatly raked ring. Ashleigh had driven up just before the class had started, and she walked around, inspecting each pony. She ran her hands over their gleaming coats, checked their feet for cleanliness, and admired the decorated manes and tails. When the grooming class was over, the riders, some with help, tacked up the ponies and then mounted. Ashleigh stood in the center of the ring as they rode around, a serious expression on her face, clipboard in hand. Yvonne announced the riders over the portable loudspeaker she'd borrowed from a friend. Those of the Pony Commandos who still needed assistance were guided around by Gregg, Janet, and Beth.

Tor showed up just as the class started their sitting trot. He leaned on the rail and encouraged the children as they walked, trotted, and cantered in both directions.

From time to time Samantha glanced at Tor, and he

grinned at her, revealing his white teeth. She felt her heart jump practically into her throat. How could he look at her like that, as if nothing were wrong? When she realized how angry she was, she decided it was time to confront him. After the show she'd make a point of seeking him out.

During the picnic lunch Tor came up and sat on the blanket next to her.

"Great job so far, guys," he said to the eager cluster of children gathered around, eating potato salad, sandwiches, and fruit. "Your ponies were well turned out, and you rode beautifully on the flat."

"Tor, did you see how my pony tried to eat the flowers in the decorations?" shrieked Charmaine, bubbling with laughter.

Tor nodded. "And you remembered what I told you about pulling up Milk Dud's head so he wouldn't engage in bad manners like that," he said.

The little girl nodded. "I did."

Samantha noticed that Mandy looked nervous, in spite of her renewed excitement about the show.

Tor must have noticed, too. "You're going to be great," he said to her.

"I still wish I could jump like you," Mandy said, looking up at her hero.

"You just keep working at it," Tor said, ruffling her black curls.

After everyone had eaten, the Pony Commandos

saddled up again for the final event of the show: the jumping. The atmosphere was tense as each Commando guided a pony around the small course that Tor had set up. When it was Mandy's turn, Samantha held her breath. The little girl sat lightly on Butterball, her thin legs in their braces clinging to the saddle girth.

"Come on, Butterball," she said. She took her reins firmly and trotted into the ring. Mandy made her first approach to the low crossrail. Leaning forward at exactly the correct angle, she urged Butterball over. She rode him around to the next jump, another crossrail, which Butterball took with ease. They went over the next few jumps smoothly, but the last, and highest, a vertical, was still to come. Mandy's face was a study in concentration as she cantered Butterball toward it. Helping him find his distance, she leaned forward and gave the chubby pony the right amount of rein. Applause exploded around Samantha as Mandy and Butterball landed squarely on the other side. Suddenly she was conscious that she'd been holding her breath during Mandy's entire go-round, and now she released it.

"She did it," she said aloud to no one in particular. She was just about to turn to Tor when she saw Angelique sidle up to the fence, smiling and waving.

"Aren't these kids cute?" she cooed sweetly in a way that set Samantha's teeth on edge.

During the ceremony, when Cindy presented horseshoes to the Pony Commandos, Samantha fought back tears.

"Great show," Tor said, putting his arm around Samantha. "I've gotta fly, but I'll see you tomorrow when I come over to work Sierra."

She stiffened and nodded. So much for confronting him. She didn't trust herself to speak. She was afraid her tears would spill out if she opened her mouth.

"What a success!" Yvonne crowed as they packed the empty coolers and baskets in the back of the car at the end of the day. "Mandy did beautifully. Did you see how proud she was when she got her horseshoe?"

Samantha took the rubber band out of her hair and fluffed out her ponytail. "Uh-huh," she said absently.

She drove home slowly. Even though the show had gone well, she felt as if there were a crushing weight on her chest. That night she tossed and turned, and the next morning, she awoke earlier than usual. She lay for a few moments looking out at the still-dark sky.

Well, she decided, it wouldn't do her any good to mope in bed. She washed and dressed, then hurried out to the stable. In the next few hours she groomed Fleet Goddess, Wonder, Sierra, and the yearlings. Len had been up all night with one of Mike's mares who'd colicked, so in addition to her usual chores she helped Cindy bottle-feed the orphans. Sitting in the

155

stall, watching the morning sun come up as the two foals nursed noisily on the big bottles, Samantha felt her sadness sweep over her in an angry wave. If only Tor still cared for her. She felt big tears well up in her eyes, and one of the foals nuzzled her.

"You're right," Samantha said in a husky whisper as she leaned against his fuzzy neck. "I'd better keep my mind on the horses. There's no use in dwelling on things I can't do anything about."

She tried not to think about Tor as she worked with Cindy and Len, teaching the yearlings to load and unload from the big Whitebrook van that had been parked in the stable yard. She'd be seeing him that afternoon when he came over to help her work Sierra. Maybe today she'd be able to say what she couldn't say the day before. Maybe they'd be able to work things out.

Samantha was leading Shining back to her stall as Len came out of the office. "Phone for you," he said.

Samantha tossed the rag she'd been holding into a dirty-laundry bag and went into the office. It was Tor on the phone.

"Hey, Sammy," he said in a hurried voice. "Listen, can you work with Sierra by yourself this afternoon? Something's come up, and I can't make it."

Samantha felt her chest tighten. *Too busy with Angelique*, she wanted to say, but she bit her tongue just in time. "Sure, no problem," she said, then replaced the phone in its cradle.

Slamming the office door on her way out, she made her way over to Sierra's stall. Sure, she could handle Sierra by herself, she thought angrily. After all, she was the one who'd ridden Sierra in the first steeplechase he'd won. She didn't need Tor, she reminded herself as she mounted the big liver chestnut and rode him over to the hedgelike fences that were set up on the turf course of Mike's training oval.

"Maybe I should just go over there and find out exactly what's going on," Samantha said to Sierra as she started him on his warm-ups. Sierra snorted, then shook his head, jangling his bit as if to say no. "Well, why not?" She sighed. "I know why not." She leaned forward, kneading her hands into Sierra's mane as she urged him into a rocking canter. It was because she wasn't just angry—she was hurt. And if she confronted him, she knew, Tor just might tell her that his feelings for her had changed. She didn't know if she could face that.

Looking toward the row of fences, she saw that Cindy was leaning up against one of the rails, watching the workout. Samantha waved, then tried to pull her mind back to the horse she was riding.

"Come on, big guy," Samantha said as she turned Sierra toward the hedge fences. "Let's show Cindy that you're ready for Saratoga."

Would Tor even show up for Saratoga at all, she

suddenly wondered. The thought so jolted her that the first fence she jumped took her by surprise. Sierra bucked as she landed on his back with a thud.

"Sorry about that," Samantha murmured to the big horse, glancing over at Cindy. She certainly wasn't setting an example for the young girl. She flew over the next fence, but the next one came up before she knew it. She tried desperately to balance Sierra, but he took off mid-stride at an awkward angle. The big horse made a valiant effort to clear the hurdle, but he had to pop over it, which jarred Samantha loose from her seat. She flew into the air, and though she landed on her shoulder, as she'd been taught, she took the full force of the fall.

"Are you okay?" Cindy yelled, rushing to her side.

Samantha held up her hand to let her know she was okay, but it took a couple of minutes before she could catch her breath and assure Cindy that she was all right. Cindy studied her with a look of concern, then took off after Sierra, who'd decided to complete the rest of the course without a rider. Samantha sat up and watched the brave horse finishing up what his rider could not. She felt a stab of shame as he trotted docilely up to Cindy after taking his last fence. Cindy looked him over for any cuts or scrapes.

"Don't worry, he's all right. You sure you're okay?" Cindy asked again. Samantha stood up, dusted herself off, and took Sierra's reins. She knelt down and ran her hands up and down the big chest-nut's legs.

"I'm okay," Samantha said. "Just bruised my pride, that's all."

Cindy's concern was replaced by a giggle. "Sorry. I know I shouldn't laugh. But Sierra looked so funny taking himself around the course with no rider."

"He loves to jump," Samantha said softly. *He doesn't deserve to be treated halfway*, she told herself sternly. She took off her helmet and sighed. Things sure weren't going her way, she thought gloomily.

The next few days didn't go any better for Samantha. Her shoulder ached like crazy, and she couldn't pull herself out of the funk she felt over Tor and Angelique.

"Here, I made you an ice pack," Cindy said. "I used to do this for the little kids at my foster home when they fell off their bikes and stuff."

Samantha smiled gratefully. "Thanks." Cindy was being so helpful, and it couldn't have been easy. They hadn't heard anything from the Child Protection Services people in several days, so nothing about Cindy's situation was certain yet.

"Maybe we could put some liniment on it, the way Vic does on the sore horses," Cindy said.

"Oh, I don't think so. It might help the horses, but it really smells bad."

That evening Yvonne called to say she was planning

a big barbecue just before Samantha left for Saratoga. "I already checked with Tor," Yvonne said casually. "He said he'd love to come."

Great, Samantha thought glumly. *He's sure not coming to see me.*

Samantha tried to concentrate as she worked Shining on the oval the next morning, but her thoughts kept drifting to Tor and Angelique. She reminded herself that Shining's first race at Saratoga was only two weeks away, and she needed to keep her beloved filly in top form and condition.

"Sammy, what's going on?" Ashleigh asked when Samantha pulled up Shining. "Shining was there for you, but you were just sitting on her back like a passenger. She didn't know what you wanted. She was frustrated and totally lost interest coming off the far turn."

Samantha took off her goggles and helmet and shook out her red hair. "I know it was a lousy work," she said wearily. "It wasn't Shining's fault. It was mine. I guess I'm just having an off day."

Ashleigh frowned. "Well, I guess everyone has an off day now and then, but I think you'd better give her another lap at a slow gallop—concentrating this time."

Samantha turned the filly. "I'm sorry, Shining. Let's do it one more time, and I'll try to keep my mind on business." She urged the filly into a collected gallop, but for once Shining didn't put her heart in it.

She knows something's wrong, Samantha thought as she tried to force herself to focus. It didn't do any good. Shining's pace was nowhere as even as Samantha knew it should be. When she pulled up at the rail and saw Ashleigh's face, Samantha knew the workout had been as bad as she thought.

The following morning's workout wasn't any better. It was clear to Samantha that Shining knew her rider's mind wasn't on business. She ran uncertainly, breaking stride by the quarter pole and then refusing to put her heart into their breeze.

"Samantha!" Ashleigh cried in exasperation. "What are you thinking about? You're going to be racing in a couple of weeks. Do you want to blow it?"

At that Samantha jerked up her head. She saw Lavinia and Brad walking up behind Ashleigh. They definitely had their timing down pat. Lavinia was grinning in wicked delight.

"That horse of yours seems to have lost her edge," said Brad in his ever-tactless way.

Lavinia chuckled in malicious glee as she looked over at Brad. "Well, I guess we don't have to worry about them at Saratoga," she said. "I told you their win was a fluke!"

Samantha felt her heart plummet into her boots. As if things weren't already bad enough, now it looked like she alone was going to ruin Shining's prospects!

"NOW, DON'T FORGET, SIX O'CLOCK SHARP," YVONNE SAID to Samantha a few days later.

"Don't worry," Samantha assured her. "I've been looking forward to your barbecue all week."

She hung up the phone just as Cindy's head appeared in the doorway of her room. "Hi," Cindy said. "Can I come in?"

By now, Samantha knew her too well. Something was up. She hoped that her dad and Beth hadn't heard bad news from the caseworker who was handling Cindy's case.

"Your dad grounded me," Cindy said unhappily. "I'm not allowed to ride for a week."

Samantha looked at Cindy. "What happened?" she asked.

"I left a gate open on the orphans' paddock,"

Cindy said. "They didn't get out, so I don't see what the big deal was. Vic saw it, and he told your dad."

"Vic did the right thing," Samantha said, opening her closet, relieved that even though leaving a gate open was a big mistake, Cindy hadn't done something worse. "Leaving a gate open can cause big trouble. What if one of the orphans got out and somehow made it onto the highway? I hate to say it, but you got off lightly if you're only grounded for a week."

Cindy scowled, but appeared to consider what Samantha said. She flopped onto the bed. "Your dad said if I messed up again, I wouldn't be allowed to go to Saratoga. So, I'm going to be a perfect angel. Are you going somewhere?" she asked when she noticed Samantha sifting through her closet.

Samantha selected an outfit, then frowned as she saw how wrinkled it was. "Yeah, Yvonne's having a barbecue. She'll be leaving for Florida to stay with Gregg's family part of the time we're in Saratoga."

Cindy sat up. "Tell me what Saratoga's like," she said. "I can't wait."

Samantha got the iron and ironing board, and while she pressed her outfit, she tried to describe the gracious old racetrack and the excitement of the meet with enthusiasm she didn't feel. She was glad that it looked like Cindy was going to be allowed to go with them. It would be a good experience for her. She remembered her first time at Saratoga, and how excited she'd been.

"I can't wait to see Shining run again," Cindy said happily before she bounded away.

I can't wait to see Tor again, Samantha found herself thinking as she turned her thoughts back to the barbecue. Tor had called her this morning in between classes. After inquiring about Sierra, he'd mentioned the barbecue, asking her if she thought he should bring anything. "I could make some of my famous chili," he said in a way that reminded Samantha sharply of the old Tor, the way he used to be, before he'd been too busy for her.

She'd told him that would be fine, and after agreeing to pick her up at five forty-five, he'd hung up, but not before he'd said, "I can't wait to see you, Sammy."

Samantha had clung to the words all day, and now, ironing her outfit, she relaxed. Maybe she'd overreacted. Maybe she was just reading too much into things she was seeing. Maybe— She jumped as the phone rang. It was Tor.

"Samantha, I'm really sorry. I just can't make it. I have to stay here and see to the horses."

Samantha was about to protest when he cut her off. "I can't talk now. Gotta go." With that, he hung up.

Samantha slammed down the receiver furiously. How could Tor do this to her? They'd planned this evening. She'd be leaving for Saratoga in a few days, and they'd hardly seen each other. Couldn't Tor spare one evening—even for a little while? She fumed a while longer as she pictured Tor sitting up with a colicky horse, or maybe tending an injury, or— A horrible suspicion crossed her mind. For once, her anger overpowered her hurt and uncertainty. She bolted down the stairs, her red hair flying behind her, and waved a quick good-bye to Cindy and her dad and Beth, who were watching TV.

"Have fun and don't be too late," she heard her dad call as she opened the door to his car.

Samantha drove quickly to Tor's stable, fueled by her growing anger. As she suspected, Angelique's sleek little car was in the stable parking lot when she pulled up a few minutes later. The light was on in the barn, and Samantha stormed down the barn aisle. Tor was carrying a couple of buckets, and Angelique came out of the hay room, carrying a huge armful of hay. She was wearing a tight black tank top that set off her gleaming blond hair magnificently.

"Should I give all of this to Zoomer?" she asked, then stopped as she saw Samantha.

"Excuse me for interrupting," Samantha said in a choked voice that sounded strange even to her ears. "But Tor, I need to talk to you." She glanced pointedly at Angelique. "Not here. Somewhere private."

Tor's blue eyes rested uncomprehendingly on Samantha for a moment. "Sure," he said in a surprised voice. "Should we go to my office?"

Samantha realized that he sounded embarrassed, but she hardly took notice as she followed him to the office, her flats slapping loudly against the concrete. Once Tor closed the door, Samantha felt herself explode. All the anger, uncertainty, and hurt of the past few weeks erupted from her.

"I demand to know what's going on," she said forcefully.

Tor stepped back.

"It's bad enough that you hardly helped out at all at the Pony Commandos' show," Samantha ranted. "And that there's no time to help me out with Sierra. You're too busy for this, you're too busy for that. But what's so important that you can't even get away from the stables for a little while to go to our good friend's barbecue?" As she talked, her voice rose higher and higher.

Tor brushed his blond hair back in a gesture that Samantha knew well, and she heard him let out his breath. "My dad's got the flu," he explained. "One of the grooms is sick, and everything just seems to be happening all at once." His eyes pleaded for understanding. "I'm sorry. I should have explained what was going on when I called, but—"

Samantha held up her hand. "So tell me, what is

Angelique doing here? If you needed help, why didn't you just call me?"

"I didn't ask her to come," he explained. "She just sort of showed up. And I've got to tell you, I needed the help."

Samantha felt her heart race as her temper took full hold. "Angelique always seems to 'sort of show up.' And it always seems that you never have time for anything except coaching her. You're never there for me anymore. That day when I saw the two of you in your office, you really acted like you were a lot more than friends, Tor."

She could see Tor's face pale as she continued, pouring out the anger and hurt that had been festering inside her. She had just taken a deep breath and was about to deliver her final shot when the office door banged open and Angelique stepped inside.

"I'm sorry to interrupt," she said, looking directly at Tor. "But I need some help. Zoomer is acting strange. I think he might be sick."

"I'll be right back," Tor said to Samantha as he headed for the door. But Samantha had had enough, especially when she saw the look of satisfaction that Angelique cast her way.

"Don't worry," Samantha said, beating him to the door. "I've said what I had to say."

She hurried to her car and slid into the driver's seat, slamming the door behind her. Starting up the car, she noticed that it was beginning to rain. "Fine," she muttered to herself. "The perfect weather to match my lousy mood." She sped off into the night, her mind whirling in confusion. Her tears flowed freely as she struggled to control the car on the slippery roads that wound their way back to Whitebrook. Her stomach started churning, and she began to wonder if she was going to be sick.

By the time she got back to the farm, the rain was coming down so hard, the windshield wipers could barely keep the windshield clear. She parked the car and glanced toward the cottage, where the lights were blazing. She just couldn't face anyone right now. Slipping in the mud as she made her way to the barn, she ducked inside Mike's office. There she picked up the phone to call Yvonne and explain that she and Tor wouldn't be coming to the barbecue.

"We had to move it indoors anyway," Yvonne said, sounding disappointed. "We'll all miss you."

It was afterward that Samantha realized Yvonne hadn't asked why she wasn't coming, and she hadn't even thought to explain.

She went to Shining's stall and leaned against her horse, burying her face in Shining's silky mane. The filly's affectionate whoofs in her ear were comforting, but even they couldn't stop her from thinking about Tor and Angelique.

She straightened as she heard Cindy opening the

door to the barn and heard her footsteps approach Shining's stall.

"Oh, there you are, Samantha," she said, stopping outside and leaning her face through the bars. "What happened? What's wrong?"

Samantha scrubbed at her face. She didn't want Cindy worrying about her. The poor girl had troubles enough of her own to deal with.

"It's nothing, really," Samantha said. "Just something I have to work out with Tor. I take it you don't have any experience with boyfriends yet."

"No," Cindy replied. "I have enough problems without them."

Samantha chuckled. "Don't worry about me. I'll be okay. Just give me a few more minutes, and I'll be back up to the cottage."

Cindy nodded and slipped away into the rainy night.

The next morning, Samantha was numb with misery. No one asked about the barbecue, and she was glad. She just didn't feel like talking to anyone. She went about her work with a leaden heart.

"He's gorgeous, isn't he?" Cindy said, sucking in her breath as she watched Len lead Pride out of the stallion barn to his paddock.

"Yeah," Samantha said softly, feeling her misery lift a tiny bit as she just looked at the beautiful stallion she'd taken care of for so long. She continued measuring Wonder's grain and special vitamins and didn't notice when Cindy slipped away after Len and Pride.

A few minutes later Samantha's head snapped up as she heard a scream, followed by the sounds of a loose horse tearing through the stable yard. She jumped up and ran from the feed room. Vic tore past her. "Pride's loose," he said. "Go around to the other side."

Instinctively Samantha snatched up a halter and lead rope from a hook, then scrambled out in the direction Vic had pointed out. If something happened to Pride after all he'd been through, she couldn't take it. Coming around the corner, she saw the magnificent horse careen toward her. He was snorting and plunging. What could have happened to upset him?

"Easy there, boy," Samantha crooned softly, never taking her eyes off him.

Pride pulled up, snorting at the sound of her voice. He tossed his head but stood still as Samantha slowly and gently eased up toward his near side.

"Come on, big guy," she said, slowly fastening the halter around him.

Len came up beside her and laid his weathered hand against the horse's trembling side. Then he gently ran his hands up and down Pride's sides to determine if he'd suffered any injury during his brief escape. "I don't know exactly what happened," he said breathlessly. "I think he might have gotten stung. I was all set to put him in the paddock when suddenly he let out a squeal and reared up. I wasn't prepared and lost my grip on his shank. Cindy tried to stop him, but he was so panicked he knocked her down. Vic's checking on her."

"Was she hurt?" Samantha asked quickly.

Len frowned worriedly. "I'm not sure."

Samantha handed Pride's lead shank to Len and darted around the stallion barn toward Pride's paddock. There she saw Cindy huddled on the ground, moaning and holding her arm as Vic knelt beside her.

"Quick," she told him. "Run to the oval and get my dad." Samantha knelt down beside Cindy in Vic's place.

"I tried to stop him," Cindy said, her face white with pain. "Is he okay?"

Samantha smoothed back Cindy's hair. "He's fine, but you're not."

"Ow, my arm," Cindy said, fat tears squeezing out of her eyes. "What if I've broken it? Will I still be able to go to Saratoga with you?"

"Let's not worry about that right now." Samantha heard her dad's boots ringing down the aisle as he strode quickly over to Cindy's side. Beth was right behind him.

"What have we here?" Beth said, kneeling down beside Cindy and assessing her arm. "We're taking you to the emergency room," she added.

Samantha helped her dad and Beth carefully lift the girl and gently help her to the car. Then she climbed into the backseat and comforted Cindy while they raced to the hospital. As soon as they arrived Cindy was whisked away, and Samantha was left in the waiting room.

Dropping wearily onto an uncomfortable plastic seat, she put her head in her hands. It had all been too much. First all the trouble with Tor. And now Cindy injured. At least Pride hadn't been hurt.

Almost an hour later Samantha's dad and Beth came through the door with Cindy. Cindy sheepishly held up her cast for Samantha's inspection. "Broke it," she muttered.

Beth put her arm around Cindy. "You just have more to learn about stallions, that's all. You tried your best. We'll think of it as a war injury."

Samantha followed them to the car, and they drove home. After they put Cindy to bed, she and Beth went to the kitchen.

"I don't know about you, but I could use a cup of herbal tea," Beth declared.

Samantha put the teakettle on and listened as Beth related the events in the examining room. "Of course, the hospital notified Mrs. Lovell right away. She implied that Whitebrook must be a dangerous place if it would allow a little girl to get so close to a 'wild stallion,' as she put it."

Samantha poured the tea and shook her head. "Pride's anything but a wild stallion," she protested.

"True," Beth agreed. "But we know how old-fashioned Mrs. Lovell is. She's absolutely convinced a horse-racing stable is no place for a young girl."

"But Cindy's doing just fine here," Samantha shot back. "She's so much happier and more secure than when she first arrived. Why can't they see that?"

"You know I agree with you, Samantha. But the whole thing is just so complicated. Who knows what will happen now?"

Samantha was staring into her teacup when suddenly she and Beth heard loud noises coming from outside. Samantha heard her father's angry tone. "On whose authority? . . . I'm not letting you take her. Why don't you think of her welfare?"

"We are thinking of her welfare." Samantha recognized Mrs. Lovell's voice. Samantha stood up as Cindy came into the kitchen, her eyes wide and frightened.

Samantha felt a chill and looked over to Cindy, whose face was white. "It's them," she gasped. "They've come to take me."

A moment later Mrs. Lovell and a uniformed officer came into the house with Ian McLean on their heels.

"Hello, Cindy," the woman said. "You've been giving us a tough time again, but we've found you a wonderful new foster home with a family in Lexington."

Cindy regarded her coldly. "I'm not going anywhere."

"You are," Mrs. Lovell said firmly. "You're going to a safe place where there aren't wild horses running around and where you won't get into any mischief."

"It wasn't Pride's fault!" she yelled. "It was mine. I just wanted to help. I'm not going!" Her voice rose to a scream. "I like it here. I want to stay here. If you make me go, I'll only run away again."

The officer knelt down in front of Cindy. "I have a court order," he said gently. "We have to obey it."

"No!" Cindy cried, tears streaming down her cheeks. "I won't go."

Mr. McLean went over to her. "I've called my lawyer," he told the distraught girl. "She's working on it right now. We want you to stay, but you'll have to go with the officer for now. We're going to straighten this out, Cindy—I promise!"

"Oh, sure," Cindy spat out. "Adults never keep their promises."

"We will, Cindy," Mr. McLean assured her.

A horrible scene followed as the officer and the caseworker loaded a screaming and crying Cindy into the back of the car. White-lipped, Beth hurriedly packed a bag with a few of Cindy's belongings. Samantha stood with her arms around her dad and

Beth as the car drove through the Whitebrook gates.

"I can't believe this is happening," Samantha gasped, tears blinding her.

"Neither can I," Beth said sadly.

"I'm going to call Ms. James again, and we're going to fight this thing all the way," Mr. McLean declared grimly before stalking off to the cottage.

Samantha walked to the mares' barn and looked in sadly at the orphans. Would Cindy ever get to see them again? It was all too horrible to contemplate. Once again she stumbled into Shining's stall and laid her cheek against her beloved horse's sleek neck.

"Oh, Shining," she moaned. "I feel so helpless."

14

THURSDAY AND FRIDAY WERE FILLED WITH TENSE AND ANX-
ious waiting. Mr. McLean's lawyer was working fran-
tically to have the court rule in his favor. Samantha
spent time helping her father, Mike, Len, Mr. Reese,
and Ashleigh fill tack boxes and collect gear for
Saratoga. It rained steadily, which did nothing for
Samantha's mood. Tor hadn't called since she'd
shown up at the stable, and she felt devastated. It
seemed to prove he no longer cared. Samantha
missed Tor and Cindy's cheerful presence so much.
Every so often she'd look in on the orphans, snug and
cozy in their stall, and she wondered if they missed
Cindy as much as she did. Whitebrook just didn't
seem the same without her.

The stable yard was a muddy mess, so Samantha,
Vic, and the other grooms walked the horses up and

down the barn aisle to keep the blood circulating through their legs. To help soothe the uptight horses, Len turned on his portable radio, and classical music flowed out mellowly through the stables. The horses seemed to like it. They nickered and shuffled contentedly in their stalls. The others talked excitedly about Saratoga, reminiscing about other good meets and other great times they had spent there. Normally Samantha would be joining them in their reminiscing. She loved the old racetrack and had wonderful memories of previous seasons.

During the worst of one of the downpours, Samantha wandered into her father's office. He was sitting at his desk, reading some papers.

"We can't go to Saratoga without Cindy," Samantha declared. She sat heavily on the sofa and started mindlessly leafing through the latest copy of *Thoroughbred Breeder* magazine.

"I have no intention of going anywhere until we have Cindy back here," her father said. "Ashleigh and Mike can go up with the horses."

Samantha looked closely at her dad. *He really cares a lot about her,* she thought. *Otherwise he'd never miss a trip with his horses to a big meet like Saratoga.* The thought cheered her somewhat. With that determination, she was sure he couldn't fail to get Cindy back somehow.

Mr. McLean looked moodily at Samantha and then

closed his books. "You know, I just might have one last idea to get Cindy back," he said thoughtfully as he stood up.

He walked out of the office, leaving Samantha to stare at his departing back and wonder what he could possibly have come up with.

Later that afternoon Yvonne braved the slick roads to come to Whitebrook. She explained that she'd been trying to call since the morning after the barbecue, but that Samantha's phone had had a strange busy signal. Over steaming mugs of instant cocoa that Samantha had made in Mike's roomy office, Yvonne bubbled about the barbecue, which hadn't been ruined at all by the unexpected rainfall. They'd just packed up everything and dashed indoors, where they'd continued to party on. Samantha listened politely, and when finally Yvonne asked her what she'd been up to, she told her about Cindy.

Yvonne was horrified. "You mean they just came and took her away, just like that?" Samantha nodded miserably. "Isn't there anything you can do?"

Samantha told her about the lawyer and what the McLeans were already doing.

"What does Tor think about all of this?"

Samantha shook her head miserably. "He doesn't even know," she said. Then, before she knew it, the whole story of Tor and Angelique came spilling out.

"I can't believe it!" Yvonne exclaimed. "You poor thing. Why didn't you tell me?"

Samantha drained the last of her cocoa. "I was hoping that maybe I was imagining things. Then I was afraid to ask Tor what was going on in case he told me he wanted to break it off between us. But you've noticed it, too, haven't you?"

Yvonne sighed and closed her eyes. "I hadn't really paid attention. I guess I was so caught up in training. But now that you mention it, yes. I know they're always training together, and she practically follows him around the stable. Oh, Sammy, I wish there was something I could do or say. And he hasn't called since the fight?"

Samantha sadly shook her head.

Yvonne put her arms around Samantha. She stayed for another hour, trying to give Samantha what comfort she could.

Samantha finished up the feeding and then checked on all the horses. It was late when she turned out the last of the lights and helped Len close up the stables. The clouds had been swept away to reveal a nearly full moon and a dark sky bright with stars. The starry night reminded Samantha painfully of another night when she and Tor had watched the stars together.

"Some kind of night," Len said, looking up at the sky. "But you're not feeling too good, are you?"

Samantha shook her head.

"Anything you want to talk about?" the old farm manager asked.

"No, Len, but thanks for asking." She felt tears well up at the old man's kindness. She honestly didn't know how she was going to get through the next days.

She turned as she heard the sound of a car coming down the Whitebrook drive. As she saw bright headlights piercing the darkness, she wondered who could be coming over so late.

She was so numb and aching, she didn't even consider the possibility that it might be Tor. He would have called long before now if she meant anything to him. She just couldn't understand how his feelings for her could have changed so quickly. Was it only the beginning of summer, after the prom, that he'd told her he loved her?

She continued walking to the cottage, then heard someone shouting her name. She turned and saw Tor rushing toward her.

"Sammy—Sammy!" he cried. "I've been trying to call you. It was a disaster at the stable. Zoomer was down with a virus, and I was afraid it might spread. I was with him for the last couple of nights. When I tried to call you, the phone lines were down. I couldn't leave the stable until the vet came and we'd checked over every one of the animals. Then my car wouldn't start. I know you must be furious, but I need to talk to you and explain."

Samantha looked at him blankly, his words hardly registering.

"There's nothing between me and Angelique," Tor rushed on. "Honestly. You're the only one I care about. I know I've been all caught up in my work lately—and I'm sorry. I'm sorry I haven't been there for you."

Samantha stepped forward, and Tor gave her a crushing hug. Then he led her to the porch steps, where he filled her in on all the events that had taken up his last few days. He'd tended the sick horse alone, since his dad and the grooms were sicker than ever. He'd sent Angelique off before the power went out. He admitted that he knew Angelique was attracted to him.

He blushed as he said, "I was flattered at first. She is pretty, and she's a top-class rider. But I never really took her seriously. I was always thinking of you, no matter how it looked." His voice softened as he added, "I guess where I made my mistake was that I didn't take the time to let you know how much I was always thinking of you."

Samantha looked down, feeling her eyes mist over for at least the hundredth time that week.

Tor went on. "Angelique was persistent. She had wanted to stay that night. But I finally came flat out and told her that I just wasn't interested. Oh, Sammy, I'm so sorry. I didn't really stop to think about how you were feeling until you let me have it."

"If only you'd told me," Samantha said.

"I know. I should have. It would have saved us a big misunderstanding. There was another part to the mess, too. I've told you about some of the business arrangements my dad and I have with our stable. We have this big backer who was threatening to sell off, and my dad's been so sick, he and I weren't able to work things out."

Samantha was aghast. "You mean you might lose your stable? Tor, that's awful!"

She moved closer and put her arms around him. After a while Samantha said, "Something awful has happened here too." She told him about Cindy.

"That's unbelievable," Tor said furiously. "Isn't the whole idea behind these agencies to help the kids?"

Samantha continued unburdening herself, telling him the whole story of how Cindy had tried to catch Pride when he got loose and broken her arm, and ending up by describing the final horrible scene with Cindy being driven off in tears.

"And if I'd had to go to Saratoga without your saying good-bye on top of everything, it would have just been too much," Samantha concluded.

"I wouldn't have let you go to Saratoga without seeing you, Sammy," Tor said, pulling her close to him. "The good news is that today my father found out that our backer has decided to stay in. That means I'll be able to spend at least a week with you in Saratoga." Tor took Samantha's hand and whispered,

"You scared me, Sammy. After you left the stable, all I wanted to do was follow you, but I couldn't leave a sick horse. I do love you, Sammy. I don't want things to be over between us."

"You scared me, too," Samantha said. She didn't want to remember how much. "I love you, Tor. Those weeks without you were unbearable. But at least they're over." She smiled up at him and leaned toward him until their lips met in a long and gentle kiss. "I just hope everything ends up as happily for Cindy as it has for us. She was doing so well here. She loves the orphans so much. If you'd seen her when they took her away . . ." Samantha's voice broke.

Tor put his arm around her shoulders and brushed loose strands of hair off her face. He kissed her again, and as they broke apart they heard an excited cry out in the yard. They jumped up to see what was going on and got to the drive just in time to see Cindy climbing out of Mr. McLean's car. She rushed toward Samantha and Tor, her face alight.

"I can stay!" she cried. "Whitebrook's going to be my home!"

Samantha and Tor caught Cindy in a three-way hug and squeezed like they'd never let go. This was truly a happy ending, Samantha thought. Cindy had come home to Whitebrook!

About the Author

Joanna Campbell, born and raised in Norwalk, Connecticut, grew up loving horses, and eventually owned a horse of her own. She took riding lessons for a number of years, and specialized in open jumping. She has published twenty novels for young adults, sung and played piano professionally, and owned an antique business. She now lives on the coast of Maine with her husband, Ian, and her two children, Kimberly and Kenneth.

☰ HarperPaperbacks *By Mail*

Read all the THOROUGHBRED books
by Joanna Campbell

#1 A Horse Called Wonder
#2 Wonder's Promise
#3 Wonder's First Race
#4 Wonder's Victory

#5 Ashleigh's Dream
#6 Wonder's Yearling
#7 Samantha's Pride
#8 Sierra's Steeplechase

And don't miss these other great horse books:

The Forgotten Filly by Karle Dickerson

When Joelle's mare, Dance Away, dies, Joelle swears that no horse will ever take her place—especially not Dance Away's filly. Then something amazing happens to change her mind. . . .

Christmas Colt by Mallory Stevens

Chrissie can't wait to get rid of her Christmas present—a scraggly colt. But as the annual auction approaches, "Klutz" develops into a beautiful yearling. Will Chrissie lose the horse she has grown to love?

And look for the complete *Across the Wild River* adventure trilogy:

#1 Across the Wild River   **#2 Along the Dangerous Trail**

#3 Over the Rugged Mountain

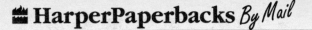 **HarperPaperbacks** *By Mail*

This collection of spine-tingling horrors will scare you silly! Be sure
not to miss any of these eerie tales.

#1 Beware the Shopping Mall
Robin's heard weird things about Wonderland Mall. She's heard it's haunted.
When she and her friends go shopping there, she knows something creepy is
watching. Something that's been dead for a long, long time.

#2 Little Pet Shop of Horrors
Cassie will do anything for a puppy. She'll even spend the night alone in a
spooky old pet shop. But Cassie doesn't know that the shop's weird owner has
a surprise for her. She can play with the puppies as long as she wants. She can
stay in the pet shop . . . forever!

#3 Back to School
Fitzgerald Traflon III hates the food at Maple Grove Middle School—it's totally
gross. Then Miss Buggy takes over the cafeteria, and things start to change. Fitz's
friends love Miss Buggy's cooking, but Fitz still won't eat it. Soon his friends are
acting really strange. And the more they eat . . . the weirder they get!

#4 Frankenturkey
Kyle and Annie want to celebrate Thanksgiving like the Pilgrims. They even want
to raise their own turkey. Then they meet Frankenturkey! Frankenturkey is big.
Frankenturkey is bad. If Kyle and Annie don't watch out, Frankenturkey will eat
them for Thanksgiving dinner.

- -

MAIL TO: Harper Collins Publishers
P.O.Box 588, Dunmore, PA 18512-0588
TELEPHONE: 1-800-331-3761 (Visa and Mastercard holders!)
YES, please send me the following titles:

Bone Chillers
❏ #1 Beware the Shopping Mall (0-06-106176-X) $3.50
❏ #2 Little Pet Shop of Horrors (0-06-106206-5)...........................$3.50
❏ #3 Back to School (0-06-106186-7) $3.50
❏ #4 Frankenturkey (0-06-106197-2).......................................$3.50

SUBTOTAL..$_____
POSTAGE AND HANDLING* ....$ 2.00
SALES TAX (Add applicable state sales tax) ....$_____
           TOTAL: ....$_____
(Remit in U.S. funds. Do not send cash.)

NAME _____
ADDRESS _____
CITY _____
STATE_____ ZIP _____

Allow up to six weeks for delivery. Prices subject to change. Valid only in U.S. and Canada.

*Free postage/handling if you buy four or more!